the international magazine of literature – issue 01

ASTRA
ECSTASY

T0030680

ECSTASY

DEAR

TO THE ANCIENT Greeks, ecstasy—
ekstasis—meant standing outside
yourself. You stand outside yourself
and a god enters you, or a new
language. You slip powder into a
water bottle and music enters you.
For me, this is what reading offers:
the chance to forget the hands that
hold the page, to inhabit the hand
that held the pen. The noise of the
subway car recedes and a story
enters. I hear the cellos in the wind
on the Wadden Sea or the scrape of
wisteria branches against a window
in Japan. As a child, I often read
while walking down the sidewalks
of Lower Manhattan. Adults scolded
me for not watching my step, but I
knew where I was going. Reading is
always traveling.

The stories in this issue will take
you from a mountain in dystopic
Kansas to a rave in the socialite
epicenter of Rio, but when we enter
another person's mind, it's always
the same distance we cross. It is
a common misconception that
international literature must be
more nutritious, more medicinal
than the writing close to home.
The most vital art is not constrained
by geography. Astra Magazine's
themes—first Ecstasy, then Filth,
then Lust—locate the subversive
emotions that run through us all.

A magazine is a community. And
there is a community—spread from
New York to Mexico City, Lagos to
Berlin, Copenhagen to Singapore,
and beyond—for which no literary

magazine yet exists. A community for whom no one place has ever quite felt like home. Our ease of travel, both physical and virtual, has disrupted space and time. Through the light of screens, we walk the streets of cities we've never visited. A fundamental truth, the one the Tower of Babel collapsed to protect, reveals itself: we can all understand one another. We share similar aesthetics and values. And while fearful governments reach toward nationalism in response, our readers reach toward each other.

Within these pages, writers of prose and poetry, cartoonists, translators, and artists enter into a conversation that rejects borders. They do not each represent a nation.

They represent an ability to stand outside and see in—into their own context, into what it means to be alive now. Their voices are as intimate as the ones in our heads, telling us things about ourselves we always knew were true, yet never had the words to name. Here you will encounter writers who have lived in many different countries, who speak through all of them, speak for none of them, who don't speak your language, yet speak directly to you.

Where do we stand when we transcend our bodies, our countries, our languages? This magazine offers a place.

—Nadja Spiegelman

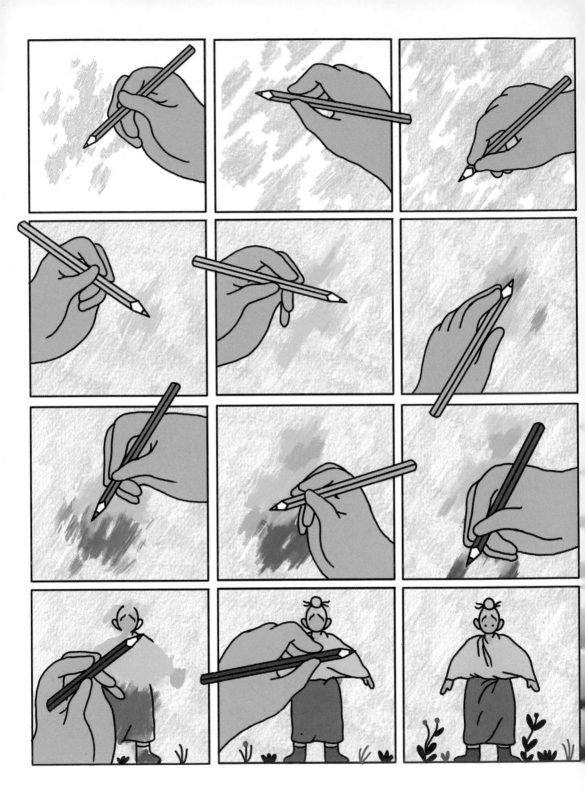

BLIND

Evan M. Cohen

Astra Magazine is published biannually by Astra House, 19 West 21st Street Suite 1201, New York, New York 10010

Printed in Canada by the Prolific Group

© 2022 Astra Magazine. All rights reserved. No part of this publication may be reproduced, stored in a retrieval system, or transmitted in any form or by any means, electronic, mechanical, photocopying, recording, or otherwise, without the prior written permission of Astra Magazine.

Distribution through Penguin Random House. If you are a retailer and would like to order Astra Magazine, call 800-733-3000 or email consumerservices@ penguinrandomhouse.com

Annual subscriptions are available. Visit https://www.astra-magazine. com/subscribe, call 888-411-9498 or email custsvc_astra@fulcoinc.com

COVER PHOTOGRAPHY: © Isabelle Wenzel, courtesy Galerie Bart PG 6 "Blind," by Evan M. Cohen was first published by Perfectly Acceptable Press in 2019. PG 58 Excerpted from LAPVONA to be published by Penguin Press in June. Copyright © 2022 by Ottessa Moshfegh. PG 122 Photographs by Eliseu Cavalcante; Courtesy of Espasso. PG 130 Copyright © 2019 Sayaka Murata All rights reserved. English translation © Ginny Tapley Takemori. Original title: Seimeishiki. Original Japanese edition published by Kawade Shobo Shinsha, Ltd., Tokyo. English language translation rights reserved to Grove Atlantic, Inc. under license granted by Sayaka Murata arranged with Kawade Shobo Shinsha, Ltd. through The English Agency (Japan) Ltd.

ASTRA ECSTASY

Editor in Chief: Nadja Spiegelman ✦

Deputy Editor: Samuel Rutter ✦

Managing Editor: Medaya Ocher ✦

Poetry Editor: Aria Aber ✦

Online Editor: Spencer Quong ✦

Creative Director: Shannon Jager ✦

Art Editor: Perwana Nazif ✦

Editors at Large: Ken Chen NEW YORK,

Patrizia Van Daalen BERLIN,

Sara Elkamel CAIRO, John Freeman LONDON,

Sonky Liu BEIJING, Daniel Medin PARIS ✦

Publisher: Ben Schrank ✦

ON THE COVER: Isabelle Wenzel, born in 1982, lives and works in her hometown of Wuppertal, Germany. She studied to be a photographer/artist, but is also a trained acrobat. The central focus of her photographs is the sculptural quality of the body, rather than the people themselves. Usually, she sets her own body before the camera. Within the seconds that the self-timer allows her, she assumes an impossible position and continues to hold it until the camera has clicked. She must carry out these acrobatic maneuvers repeatedly in order to realize an image. In this way, Wenzel enacts an experimental performance piece in front of the camera, then captures it for us frozen into a photograph.

HOUSE PARTY
Katharina Volckmer
ILLUSTRATION BY Sawako Kabuki

IT WASN'T EASY to get invited to your housewarming party. Or rather to get my colleague with the ridiculous mustache invited, so that I could come along under the pretense of a fetish for his facial hair. You know how he always goes on about his alleged Athenian grandfather, and how he takes pride in the European nature of his curls. Recently he even started wearing a golden necklace to prove his point and I wonder when he is going to start speaking with an accent. It's all gotten worse since you left the company and I'm still wondering why exactly people enjoy growing pubic hair on their faces. I have always much preferred your clean look, with your skin so tender and fragile. Like something that needs rescuing, something that is not unfamiliar with the outer edges of despair.

After all those months without seeing you, when I finally followed my colleague and his mustache into your newly converted flat, I was ready to offer comfort. Just like in the past, I had come up with countless scenarios for how to turn our acquaintance into something steamy. Into pure drama and passion. My life would suddenly matter because we would start holding hands on a train. Or because we would survive some drastic violence and suddenly discover our love among transformative amounts of adrenaline. Or I would discover a hidden talent and, overcome by admiration for my professional endeavors, you would find even the traces of my body irresistible. I dreamed about finally being able to touch your hair. Those thick light brown strands that always look like you have just returned from a holiday. That are strong enough to be pulled. I dreamed about being close to you. About sharing something that could count as a bodily experience in the hope that my dignity would one day step in and meet my longing at dawn. Because it's not like your

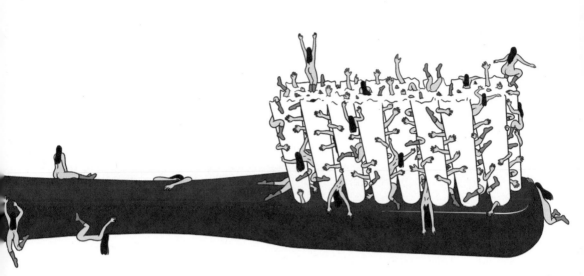

appeal was universally acknowledged before you inherited all that money from your strange aunt. When we were still working together, some people even made fun of your tote bags and your tendency to correct their pronunciation. They said you look like someone who smiles in the rain.

I don't know what exactly is living inside my mouth. Bacteria they say. Little creatures that make me an entity, that protect me against the world and cause bad breath. I wonder if they have legs, if they go dancing on their day off and where they bury their dead. Do they send the residue of their existence down my throat, into the darkness of my bodily functions? There are days when I would like to meet them, to hear what they have been up to, whether they agree with my choice of toothpaste and what they think of my new electric brush. Do the rotating bits of plastic soaked in foam fill them with pleasure? Does it make them feel like children that are allowed to stay in their seats during a car wash? And what do we mean when we talk about bad bacteria? When we pretend that there are morals affecting our bodies. I remember the stains the insects used to leave behind on our windscreen—red and yellow—their matter and their fluids joined in the kind of fingerprint that has now become so rare. That I now long for on my clean journeys through concrete landscapes. And I wonder whether the creatures inside me get smashed in similar ways, whether my flesh is colored by the remains of their opposition. Or are they too small for my violence? Maybe it's always been the trick not to be bigger but smaller than the thing that is trying to kill you. To have a heart that is too small to break.

But it's too early to talk about broken hearts. The plural seems like an exaggeration. Even I know that the hearts of the deluded suffer on their own.

I can't even claim your rejection because I've never offered you my affections. My pain has its roots in an unacknowledged situation because you don't know that I think about you before I fall asleep and it's just as well that you married someone who knows how to decorate things, someone with solid aesthetics. Someone who makes you look happy in the midst of all those smooth objects and the seamless transitions that exist between them. Content in the knowledge that you live inside a picture, that the two of you have somehow managed to fuck your telephones and give birth to this isle of wonders. That all this fake pottery is going to outlive us all. Remnants of stoneware made in Portugal scattered across empty plains and, in the background, wild things multiplying without effort. Even when we are long gone, the remaining flora will still be seen playing with bits of our universal color palette. But your offspring won't be part of this, and neither will that dog that you are so inevitably going to adopt. The gatekeeper to your indestructible happiness. The cherry on top of your fucking cake. I can already tell, by that suspicious gap in your interior design, that their bed will be in the corner by the floor lamp and their little jacket on a hook in the corridor, only a short distance away from your own layers.

In the morning, one of you will chat to other dog owners while pretending that the park is the countryside and therefore requires special outfits. That those bits of green can be conquered only in special footwear, reveling in a bit of mud while forcing the dogs to stay clean. Forcing them to wear fabrics on top of fur to prevent them from doing their unpleasant dog things. Stopping them from rolling around in shit and dead rats. Bringing them even closer to becoming walking toys, the lead dancers in our desire to defeat all meaning. I can see you, the ease with which you wear your clothes. Only expensive things can be worn so carelessly, and it pains me to witness your decline into the realm of aesthetic comfort. I miss those days when you would wear baggy shorts in the summer and roll your own cigarettes, when you also had to deal with broken boilers and cheap food before payday. When it was less unlikely that we could have been friends. And I miss the rumors about the things you got up to in the office after those horrid staff parties. The knowledge various people possessed of different parts of your body.

Now, I fear that you might even buy a boilersuit and give yourself artisan airs, the occasional fleck of paint and confusion in your hair, a small part of your flat turned into a studio where you make trousers or taxidermy butterflies. I wish I had the means to buy you an ugly couch. Or to take a knife to your perfect wallpaper and carve out my desire, to be sick in your expensive palm tree and find a color that would bring out the ugliness in your perfection. But your partner has watchful eyes. His talent for hostility far exceeds that of your future dog. He is not an eternal puppy, not one of those comfort things that people buy alongside their dildos. I'm sure he would be reliable in the event of a calamity. I can see him lifting heavy things or dealing with burglars but beyond that, I see nothing. Just his silent anger and his muscular existence, but none of the juicy bits, nothing that makes life feel like orchids will spring from the corners of your wounds and losses. Nothing about him signals a future without defeat and when I look at his flawless shirt, I can feel an absence of poetry. But maybe that's why you chose him, to hide behind his shape, to make him do the things you don't want but that you still desire. Maybe it was like voting for a conservative party, with that little moment of faith in a better version of ourselves before all idealism is washed away by personal advantages. In his shadow you can carry on living your ridiculous life and find comfort in the contrast between your worlds. Because after all, you're rich now and you couldn't have shared your life with someone who doesn't dream of clean sheets. He is your ticket to looking like you belong where you landed. And maybe this means that you won't actually have to change, that you can let him plant the bee-friendly flowers and buy the supplements but that you still get to lick the paper of your own cigarettes. Just to remind yourself that your lips have not forgotten how to move.

And so I just spend my time feeling nervous, trying to admire what my heart despises, unable to get any closer to you. Or your hair. Or the sensations my body produces when you are near, the spark that undoes my desolation and makes me want to reach for the edges of your fine garments. To reach for that slender body of yours that I imagine soft like the inside of a good pear, and that you still hide beneath white T-shirts. Though now it looks like you wash your colors separately. And you are suddenly so popular in these social situations, people now flock to you as if there were precious things coming out of your holes. I don't think we will be able to talk for more than a few minutes. Someone will start standing next to you, waiting for the right moment to interrupt, pushing me off the back of that boat and leaving me to drown in my visions of what could have been. I'm not even sure what it is about you, apart from your sudden wealth. Maybe it's because your foreignness comes from an attractive place and they like to soak in the allure of a fancy otherness? Or maybe they are also partial to your luscious locks. Or maybe you have turned your bookishness into something more exclusive, now that you can afford to be a little ridiculous. You might even have told people that you are working on a novel and they forgave you and found it endearing. And they don't even mind that you always claim to know things before everyone else, as if angels filled your dreams with novelties. But I doubt they know about your other side, about your erotic potential. They wouldn't have looked deeper into those sullen eyes of yours to discover your hidden kinks. The things that I think we should do together. The things that the creatures in my mouth would enjoy, because they felt it, too. Because when we smell something, we breathe in little particles and the creatures distinguish between fractions of flowers and fractions of other people. Between the things that give pleasure and those that don't. And we could taste your perfume as soon as I walked into the room.

Initially, I was worried about how they would react to strangers. There are so many theories about the things that other people's bacteria do to our bodies. Apparently, a new sexual partner makes your skin go itchy, but I wouldn't know because my sexual partners are always new and never last long enough for my skin to form an attachment. All I know is that my thoughts leave my skin looking somewhat stained and unappealing, like the bark of a sycamore tree struggling with pollution. My skin doesn't look like something that would inspire romantic thoughts. Something people would like to caress and care for. Something that contains a future. And still I dream about your hands, their skin always a little too dry and your pinkies looking so frail, as if they belonged to someone else. I can feel your hands even now, moving between my legs, their rough surface rubbing against my softer tissues. As my desire sends all my blood to hold your fingers tight, as we stand in the door of your study and you look at me with those motionless eyes, knowing exactly when to stop. When my pleasure is about to overcome itself. Because in my mind you are more exciting than gentle and without taking those eyes off me you free your fingers and move them to my lips. Making me lick clean what I so gladly sullied. And I know that our private parts have powerful bacteria, that they act as a shield against the world and might well have killed all the danger you brought to my mouth.

I can feel your partner's small eyes on me as I look toward the doorframe I want us to lean against. He might even notice the force with which I'm holding on to my wineglass. How its delicate bits are about to surrender to my diverted lust. And I realize that it's time for me to pretend I'm here with my colleague and his ridiculous mustache, but he is probably busy telling people about the intricacies of traditional Greek cuisine and I suddenly feel like I have no real reason to be here, like I'm looking at this party from within the walls of an aquarium. Unable to make myself heard, a solitary idiot floating in a landscape that's only a replica of what other people think of as real. A castle is a joke if the entrance is as big as your own head, and everybody knows you haven't achieved very much if you are dependent on someone else making sure that a mixture of algae and your own shit doesn't kill you. The other people at this party clearly think I'm not worth talking to because my brain is not capable of producing any relevant feelings, because I use my lips to suck the walls of my own prison and I breathe through a part of my body most of them couldn't even name. Yet my gills make me vigilant and at least I don't look like I'm mostly breathing through my arse. I know that there is beauty in my invisible parts, but your partner is the only one who sees me. He's the only one who can tell that I have feelings that don't belong. And still, I defy him. Because just as a fish has the right to disappear into the background, to inhabit the ridiculous castle, so I have the right to use your bathroom. To find gold beneath the shop-bought sand. Even though your partner looks like someone whose farts sound like whip cracks, he's hardly in a position to regulate my physical needs. His small eyes follow me as I leave my wineglass on the sofa table and they only give up once your bathroom door is firmly locked behind me. The sound of the latch drives away my predator's gaze.

I don't remember much about your bathroom, except that it made use of some daring wall paint and otherwise seemed to compete with ambitious levels of hotel perfection. It was the kind of bathroom where all traces are immediately visible and I was reminded that it takes this kind of flat to look like a decent person in the morning. That these bathrooms actually exist in

London. There was even a plant, not some kind of plastic orchid from a restaurant toilet, but a real plant. And I thought of all the things the plant had witnessed from that angle where it could see the toilet as well as the bathtub. It was probably more familiar with you than your partner and I hope it will treat my little secret with kindness. We don't think of intimacy as an act of hygiene but rather as a somewhat joyful moment of contamination. I like to think of it like that, I'm sure the creatures in my mouth would agree. They seem to enjoy the special freshness they have been blessed with ever since, that I can still feel when my tongue touches my teeth. But I had to turn my back to the plant, I wasn't sure if it could be trusted, whom its heart belonged to. Then there was, of course, the decision about which one was yours: they were both the same color, stuck in those elegant Japanese holders. But I found it quite easy. Your partner is a meaty type who could easily chew through difficult textures and so I figured that his must be the brush with little bits of food stuck between the bristles while yours was spotless and had suffered from less force. I put some of your enamel-supporting toothpaste onto your brush and put it in my mouth. It was sweet like the toothpaste from my childhood when I would sometimes sneak into the bathroom to eat bits of it, and the creatures danced to the rhythm of my strokes, the foam growing until I finally felt close to you. I brushed very slowly, the way I imagined you would move your fingers between my legs. I could even feel how big your fingers would be inside my mouth and every time your brush was about to come out, my teeth locked gently to keep it in its place. Like an animal biting with excitement. And I think I smiled as I looked in the mirror and imagined that this could really be us, that you could come in at any point and finish what I started. That I could finally surrender to your movements. But all pleasure is finite and as I felt the foam dripping from my mouth, my lips budding with bliss, the sweetness of the paste had turned into a sting, alerting me to the dangers of overdosing on fluorides. And so I bent over and relieved myself into your sink, lovingly taking in your tap as I washed my mouth before burying my face in your tumble-dried towels. Sunshine touching my face on a Friday night. I knew then that it was time to leave because unlike your future dog, your partner would be able to smell my unsuitable freshness, could see me smile with all the things that lived inside me and he wouldn't forgive me, no matter how gentle I had been with your brush. And as I exit your bathroom I get a glimpse of you in your study, you have been cornered by my colleague and his ridiculous mustache. You look tired, there are lines showing on your forehead but if I'm not mistaken you are actually interested in what he's got to say. You care about the different ways of preparing *loukoumades* and I realize that you will soon start making your own bread. That you will start wearing your hair short and start believing in happiness. That I have had the best of you and that it would be a mistake to let the reality of you conquer my delusions. As I head for the door, I can feel your partner's small eyes on me again, but this time I let him look. This time I feel what he will never find the words for. And I leave with the sensation of another man's hunger on my skin, my own sorrows suddenly lifted by the wings of a lighter fate. ✦

THINGS SEEN RIGHT & LEFT WITHOUT GLASSES

Terrance Hayes

Sometimes I feel like a motherless town
full of fathers who get custody of their sons
in the divorce, a town of hotels and campers
and men and boys who speak as strangers

but feel the blood they share.
I remember the policeman arrested the child
after hitting him so hard, his face caved
in the nightmare and the sound woke me.

My cry can be heard if you lay an ear
to my Adam's apple, named so as proof
it was Adam who tried to swallow
where Eve only tried to bite the fruit.

Everything said and unsaid, issues from us
like a humming like honey clogging the pipes
with sweetness. Sometimes I feel like dancing.
We gonna dance the night away.

Sometimes I feel like somebody's watching me.
Sometimes I feel like I got to run away.
Sometimes I feel like the child whose disfigured
expression was placed in a fishbowl.

Why would anyone ever truly want to relax?
Where I'm from everybody fights everybody
to get to truly know them. I plan to change
my mind according to intuition's Venn diagram

of the people who know the truth overlapping
with people who don't know the truth
overlapping with people who know the truth
but lie about it overlapping with people

who don't know the truth but think they do.
We're in the colorful gray between up and down.
Have mercy, I hear you say. It may not be
right or wrong. It may not be true or false.

Sometimes I feel like someone who parks
with the headlights facing the road.
Sometimes I feel like someone who parks
with headlights facing the house.

Not so much the tongue as its negotiation
with the throat and teeth. Not so much a muscle
as a space for mediating the bite and swallow.
As if the spine is a hollowed bony pole with teeth

around a throat attached to the gastrointestinal tract
attached to the anus. Sometimes I feel like Alice
proves nothing's wrong with a rabbit hole.
There must be a place to process what is taken in

and what is released. Throw your hands in the air
and wave like you're changing a light bulb.
Remember the first time you stayed up past midnight
like someone who was almost a know-it-all?

© Trine Søndergaard, Strude #1, 2007-2010, courtesy the artist and Martin Asbæk Gallery

WADDEN SEA SUITE
Dorthe Nors

Translated from the DANISH by CAROLINE WAIGHT
PHOTOGRAPH BY Trine Søndergaard
MAP BY Aaron Reiss & Larry Buchanan

IT'S DARK IN Huisduinen, south of Den Helder, in the Netherlands. I hear from Denmark that the first storm of autumn is drawing in from the North Sea, bringing winds of hurricane strength. It's due to hit the northwest coast back home. I told my dad over the phone that I was going to the southernmost edge of the Wadden Sea, the vast, enigmatic tidal sea on the Dutch, German, and Danish coastlines, and he decided my timing was poor.

"But I'm about five hundred miles away from your storm," I replied, because he's often worried about people going about here and there. His West Jutlandic roots have a solid hold on him that way. Watching what you say and talking people back into place when they're a tad too keen to move are normal in the West Jutlandic hinterland. The coast is for those lured by the foreign. They've no good soil, so they're quite a sorry lot. But two miles farther in, we reach the hinterland. The hinterland is for those with money in real estate and profitable earth. They come down hard on wanderlust. Say you're at some Christmas market in the hinterland with your gingerbread, and you're making conversation at a stall that sells hand-knitted socks:

"So what are you up to these days?" the saleswoman asks you.

"I'm just back from London, actually," you might say.

"London?! Oh, but that's ghastly," the saleswoman says. "And you do look a sorry little thing," she might decide to add.

Big cities, free speech, and foreign lures are the work of the devil. All three are a threat to the existing order. The word bonde, Danish for farmer, comes from Norse, and means "settled man." A settled man is master in his own house and reluctant to move.

What the women are, the dictionary of the Danish language neglects to mention. Still, one thing is for sure: a person glad to seek out other regions is a defector, an overløber, which comes from the German Überläufer, and describes a person who has gone over to the enemy. Any time you say you've been to New York, Berlin, or Cairo, what you're really telling the hinterlander before you is that you don't think he or she is good enough. My dad's got this same conditioned reflex from his proud West Jutlandic forebears. One of the times he was most frustrated over my urge to see exotic places was when I moved to Fanø, in the Wadden Sea. Fanø is an island, and people who live in such places are encircled by water. That means wanderlust, no question, and anyway, water is dangerous. Ships go down. Ferries, too. My risk of drowning rose considerably, he felt.

But I lived on Fanø for a year. It was unforgettable. I was besotted with a married man. The married man was besotted with me being besotted with him, and it should have set all the lighthouses along the coast to flashing, but it didn't. He lived far away, I lived in the village of Sønderho at the southern tip of the island, and with every day that passed I was swallowed up more and more by the landscape. The Wadden Sea is powerful, and I lived a far stretch out there. You don't come out the other side unchanged.

First, I stayed at Julius Bomholt's House, also called the Poet's Home, a big old shipmaster's house owned by Esbjerg Council. It is made available to Scandinavian writers as a retreat and was mine for six months. But when it came time to move out, I wasn't done with Fanø. I had an extended trip to the U.S. coming up. The married man was involved. I thought I might as well stay in Sønderho until then, so I took a room with a lovable local woman in her shipmaster's house. Johanne's House, I call it in my memories, because that's what it was: her house.

My year in Sønderho is a cello's sound inside me. I have only to glimpse the chimneys of Esbjerg Power Station and it begins to play. It sounds like an old-fashioned piece, Bach or Pärt. The silent space, a lonely string instrument, and then that long-suffering bending to the wandering of the moon and the clock of the tides. I love the Wadden Sea, though there's something strange and sucking about it, and so I got a train from Amsterdam to Den Helder. There I rented a bike, despite the gusting wind. I wanted to get to Huisduinen and see the sign that marks: here begins the Wadden Sea. If you can say that something so strangely ethereal begins, and you can. You can see with the naked eye where that force takes over. In Denmark the transition is strongly felt along the west coast of Fanø and up toward Skallingen; the infinitely slick and grooved expanses pass from the south into something like a sea, lined with nearshore breakers. Nearshore breakers: the North Sea. Wide-flung tidal flats: the Wadden Sea.

Cycling to Huisduinen, I saw the transition there, too. Sand flats, lying in readiness, gigantic bars in the agitated water. This is where it begins, then: the Wadden Sea UNESCO World Heritage Site. The national park ends somewhere north, up by Johanne's House, and I wanted to see this miracle take over from a southern direction.

"You don't want to walk smack into a spinning top like that," said my dad on the phone.

"But I'm so far from the storm," I said. "It's up near you lot. Not here."

But storms have eyes. Their eyes are round, and they whirl. Grand Hotel Beatrix in Huisduinen has taken me into its fold. The hotel is located immediately behind the dam, a burly asphalted hulk, and on the other side of the northbound highway is the lighthouse, Lange Jaap, casting its bright cone into the pelting rain and sea foam. There is a storm blowing in Huisduinen. Lange Jaap sharpens and resists. Everything is black besides the light, sweeping rhythmically across the hotel. I've taken cover in my room. The building shakes. Small fox in the cave's darkness.

Still, I did my best to make it to the dam before nightfall. I walked south with a scarf over my face. Grains of sand stinging, eyes watering.

I walked like a slash against the wind while the sea toiled against the disaster-proof dam. To the north, Den Helder, which so oddly mirrors Esbjerg back home, and a ferry bravely making the short crossing to the island beyond the town. It could have been Fanø, but it was called Texel. It's the southernmost of the Frisian Islands, and Fanø is the northernmost. Island sisters, and I would have been there, but had to settle for seeing it at a distance. And finding the sign, and I found it:

WELKOM IN HET WADDENZEE
WERELDERFGOED GEBIED

WELCOME TO THE WADDEN SEA
WORLD HERITAGE SITE

It's warm here in the Beatrix. I've taken out a map. I'm looking at islands with funny names. To the south are the West Frisians, Texel the first pearl in the chain—or the pot of gold at the end of the rainbow. After Texel come Vlieland, Terschelling, Ameland, Engelsmanplaat, Schiermonnikoog, Rottumerplaat, Rottumeroog, and then the islands known as East Frisian: Borkum, Juist, Norderney, Baltrum, Langeoog, Spiekeroog, Wangerooge, Mellum. They speak German now, call themselves North Frisian, and keep adding and adding, like pearls on a string. Then Pellworm, Hooge, Amrum, Nordstrand, Gröde, Langeness, Oland, Föhr, and Sylt. The language transforms slowly with each pearl, and suddenly they speak Danish. They call themselves Rømø, Mandø, Fanø, Langli.

The chain is intact. No border can sever it.

It ought to be silent here, I think, under the duvet, listening to the fury outside. Silence and a stringed instrument.

The Wadden Sea is one large violin body that the water plays a few times a day, rising and falling, rising and falling. That's how I pictured it the year I lived there. This silent suite was broken only by the fire alarm. In Sønderho on the southern tip of Fanø, the alarm went off at noon every single Saturday. For there are three things they fear in Sønderho: shipwrecks, storm surges, and fire. The town of shipmasters is thatched. Each house, except for a few lone contrarians, is orientated east to west. And thatched. Around them a system of paths and orchards. The idyll is absolute, Grade I listed. So every Saturday at noon, the fire alarm went off. That way you knew it worked should all hell break loose.

And then came the women. Since the siren was going off at twelve every Saturday anyway, they thought they might as well use it as a signal to summon the tribe. They slipped out of their gloriously painted shipmasters' houses. They walked down Landevejen and Nord Land, Øster Land, Sønder Land, Vester Land. They darted, scurried, and strode down tangled paths through Sønderho, paths laid down by the coffee-thirsty. They steered a course for the pub, where a long table was set out for them. The stocks of draft beer and white wine had been kicked up a notch. The coffee machine was switched on and the Brøndum Snaps was laid out (Rød Aalborg is for the mainlanders) because there had to be booze-laced coffee, too, to keep everything going. And there they sat, the women of Sønderho. They settled their broad backsides around the table, becoming their own version of fire. Gossip set ablaze.

A kind of matriarchy, yes. Historically speaking, a small community where women held power. When the people of Fanø bought their island from the king in the mid-eighteenth century, they also bought their freedom and the right to international sea trade. They didn't need to be told twice. In Sønderho, the men purchased big ships, declared themselves shipmasters, and set out like the Frisians they were to trade across the seven seas. They got a long

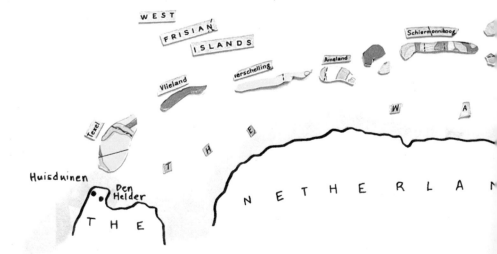

way, the men of Fanø. They brought riches home. The shipmasters' houses grew, flourished, acquired fantastical colors, garrets, windowpanes, and extensions. Sønderho transformed into a miraculous village, a community at once isolated and international, in the middle of a wayward sea. Sometimes the men were away for months. Other times they set out on long voyages and were away for years at a stretch before they came home. If they did come home, that is, for ships go down. And here's how the situation worked out for Sønderho's women:

Your husband is at sea most of the time. When he comes home, if he comes home, he gets you pregnant. On top of that, he must be occupied somehow. If he's busy painting the outside of the house, he won't be underfoot inside. So you put him to work.

"Why don't you paint stripes above the windows, my friend," you say.

It takes time, and meanwhile, everything carries on much as before. You're used to running things. You farm. Keep animals. You, the children, the other women, and the old men help one another when he's away.

Sometimes you go, too. Sometimes you join your husband, your brother, your father, and see the world. But back home, it is you who decides when the hay should be harvested.

This is how it was. They settled things for themselves, the women, by and large. Decisions great and small, including those on behalf of the village—they took care of it all. Which was fine, and she looked forward to him coming home. Even though it was a hassle, his restlessness, the power struggles, and uncertainty. Four or five such years can turn a spouse into a stranger, near enough. And again, he had to be off. Gather, scatter. Gather, scatter.

If he did not come home—that, too, was dreadful. Then she was a widow in a village of many widows and unmarried women. But the widows and the spinsters moved in together. They took care of one another and the children. They drew an ingenious system of paths between the houses of the elderly with their feet. A cottage industry sprang up, dealing in mutual care, preserved fruit, salted fish, gossip, social control, and money. While the straightening of the river Skjern shows what a landscape looks like when someone's been at it with a level, you should look at Sønderho to see how paths arrange themselves under women's feet: organic as the roots of trees.

The sign of Fanø's matriarchy was their dress. Fanø's men just wore clothes: wooden shoes or boots, wadmal, and a cap. But Fanø's women wore a uniform. It didn't emerge out of thin air—it emigrated from the south, like their architectural style, their genes, their merchant zeal. In other words: it was Frisian. If you disregard the trading town of Ribe, where you could sell your fish, Fanø was more orientated downward, toward its sister islands, than toward the Danish mainland.

At the top of the uniform was a scarf simply called a cloth. Its bow had to be knotted in a particular way that made it look like a sail. Frisian woman: sailor wife. There was no shortage of skirts because it was important to create wide hips underneath a narrow waist. The jacket was buttoned up if you were unmarried. If you were married, a single button was left undone. There were various versions of the garments appropriate for various phases of life. Little girls learned at around seven years old to tie their cloths, initiating them into the tribe. The women's garb was roughly the same color as the houses, so in principle he was also mending her if he came home. And if he came home, they danced together. They danced one of the most beautiful traditional dances on Earth: the sønderhoning.

It really has to be seen, but this is how it goes: First they walk hand in hand, then he reaches both his hands around her, behind her back. Putting one of her arms behind her back, she grabs hold of his arm. The other arm she places lightly around his body. Then they whirl like scaled-down dervishes across the floor. They have each other caught by a centrifugal force. Like a North Sea depression, with its silent eye and its wildness at the periphery. He clasps her firmly, as though she were life itself. She allows it, and looks determinedly, not coyly, at a slanted angle to the floor. For he has a solid grip on her, the man, but he does not own her.

The first time I saw a young couple spontaneously take to the floor and dance the sønderhoning at a pub one chance night when someone happened to have brought their violin, I was moved.

"Oh, that's just beautiful," I said to the others at the table, who then got up and danced, too, as though it were quite an ordinary thing to do at the end of the world one weekday night: to dance a dance so simple and powerful that it has survived for generations. The young people look like it comes to them naturally. I don't know if that's true, because it's difficult, and where I come from we were forced to dance traditional dances at the community center, after which we immediately forgot them. There's a community center in Sønderho, too, where they might have been made to learn, so maybe somebody pushed them through it. But as adults, they look like they wanted to dance of their own accord. I tried, but the man I could have danced with was absent, and anyway he had committed to dancing with somebody else.

I wonder how Texel, beyond the hard-boiled dam and the water, feels about the mainland. Was it, like Fanø, reasonably indifferent until it was reduced to a place for vacationers and romantics from the capital? Are they still full of wanderlust over there? Opportunistic, die-hard, self-assured? Does the Wadden Sea tug at them the way it tugged at me the year I lived in Sønderho, still young and full of illusions? It affected you, the Wadden Sea and its tidal pulse. The natives knew that. Births got underway as waters rose, they said. Those due to die died when the waters receded. You could read it in the obituaries. So-and-so died late Tuesday night "at falling tide." That was important to include. God was one thing, the Wadden Sea was another, and the two things could scarcely be separated.

I used to walk down Nord Land every night, up to the dike, listening. The starry sky formed a dome above the island, vast, curved, and infinite. As I stood there, I sensed the depth of this curve. Up and down became relative terms, and when I shut my eyes, I could hear the silence of the Wadden Sea, like some kind of resonance. North, the sound of breakers taking over. A deep bass sound of currents and snapping water. But to the south and southeast were the flats, and through the flats ran the enormous underwater trenches, the deeps. These channels and their tributaries, the tideways, ran like juicy veins into the mudland.

Unseen, almighty, they wove quietly in and out, in and out of the Wadden Sea, like blood supplying a placenta. The deepest trenches had been given names, the seriousness of which was understandable—Knot Deep, Gray Deep, Gallows Deep—and the Wadden Sea became a huge basin beneath the vaulted stars, where everything fertile grew, including death. Perhaps the cello's sound was coming from the deeps, from the tideways. Perhaps I'd brought it out there myself. Perhaps it couldn't be any other way.

The lighthouse rakes its beam across the sea, and I have set the map of the Frisian Islands aside. I'm looking at old photographs from Fanø instead. It's safe that way, and what I see in the pictures is the way they carry themselves in nearly all of them, the women. Wrapped in cloths, padded, wide-hipped by their underskirts. Their jackets narrow across their chests, their faces hard as leather. They stand at one end of the house, gazing confidently at the interloper.

These are Johanne's foremothers. They stand in front of sand dunes, swollen orchards, and buses. Johanne once told me that her ancestors were Frisians from the south who had settled on Fanø sometime in the seventeenth century. They'd been living on the island so long that her grandmother, as a child, had been painted by the well-known Fanø artist Julius Exner. The portrait hung in Johanne's living room. Grandma as a little girl, with a pretty cloth, already initiated into the tribe. As I recall, there was a cat in her arms as well. Inside the wardrobe, the grandmother in the painting rose from the dead in the form of traditional Fanø clothing: the clothing Grandma had worn when she became a grown woman. To Johanne, the clothing was sacred. Every year on Sønderho Day in July, people told her she should put it on. She didn't want to. She didn't like the way the mainlanders and vacationers, slightly too rich and privileged, played dress-up in her foremothers' costumes. The garments were deeply serious, and not just something to wear for carnival one day out of the year. They were dolling themselves up in borrowed plumage, Johanne felt, and on the whole, I thought she was right. The last Fanø woman to regularly wear the clothing died in the seventies. The exodus from the outer periphery to the big cities had begun. The era of the shipmasters was long over, and so was the matriarchy. From now on, the women were supposed to have children to keep the local community alive. The young women on Fanø started to wear miniskirts and bell-bottoms; they styled their pageboy haircuts with curling irons. They were wrapped up in the number of pregnancies, both theirs and other people's: the survival of the school, of the greengrocer. But the city slickers wanted to have their fun with the passing of time: they played at the old days, marched in processions through the city with cloths bristling and hips rolling. Johanne, sweet person that she was, put up a quiet resistance. Grandma's clothing was not to be sullied by vapid tourism or people who didn't understand what it meant.

For it meant more than just power. It meant longing, hard graft, vulnerability. And it meant that you lived with the Wadden Sea, in birth and in death. That you realized what those great flats gave—life and rich growth, wildfowl, glasswort, amber—and what they took from human life. Grief came with the privilege of wearing the clothes, and coffee laced with schnapps wasn't just about standing one's ground stoically against the cold. It was also medicine to combat the forces of Gallows Deep.

In the storm outside, between Texel and Den Helder, are the underwater rivers of Marsdiep and Het Nieuwediep, and somewhere near the harbor you might run across a pumping station called De Helsdeur—Hell's Gate. They understand, the West Frisians, that this landscape is bountiful one minute and all-consuming the next. It is the job of Hell's Gate to try to keep hubris at bay. I hope it holds tonight while I look at pictures. There's one of a Fanø woman by her neat picket fence. There's one of a Fanø woman with her daughters in tow. There she stands where she can, and she's in the center. In one of the pictures, you sense this woman's presence to an almost supernatural degree. It was taken on Fanø Beach one February day in 1915. A group of women in Fanø dress have gathered like cormorants in the cold. Maybe they're posing for the photographer, their cloths fluttering in the wind. Maybe they're making sure nobody gets any closer. Behind them is an enormous sagging German zeppelin by the name of *L3*. It has just been on fire, and as the women stand there, they seem to be keeping watch over the burning. Only the day before, this zeppelin had been a giant, making its way from Hamburg to Skagerrak to scout for British submarines. There was a war on, of course. And then came the southwest storm. It set in with snow. The zeppelin drifted in the wind, the engines battling to no avail. Half an hour north of the German border, the last one gave out. An emergency landing in neutral territory on Fanø was their only resort. From the safety of the beach, the Germans shot a flare into the airship, setting it alight. Flames and curiosity had drawn these women. They are of another world, standing there. No, they were of another world.

I don't know what Johanne thought when the fire alarm went off every Saturday, gathering the women of Sønderho at the pub for a drink and a gossip. I think she thought it was nice. She used to go along, at any rate. At Johanne's house, I'd often sit and chat with her about anything and everything. Even after I left the island, came home from the U.S., and moved to Copenhagen. My wanderlust took over. The schism in which all identity is formed made me set out.

The water rose and fell, the pulse beating the hours of the day. I know that good souls around Johanne eventually prevailed upon her to wear her grandmother's clothes, just for one day of carnival. If anyone was going to wear it, she should be the one. And she was proud of it, after all, she told me on the phone. She'd felt strong and beautiful in it, and I wish I could have seen her. But I never did. The last time I visited Sønderho, it was for Johanne's funeral. That day no one wore Fanø dress, but the grief, that was real.

At coffee after the funeral, we sang the song that's always sung at gatherings on Fanø. Gather, scatter. A song that mimics the tides and the comings and goings of the world. A people with wanderlust aren't afraid to sing in chorus, "The time has come to travel, friend—my path to distant lands I wend."

To that song, my hinterland family would have moaned, "Ghastly." In their circles, they sang, "The Jutlander, he's strong and tough, and he will not be moved." But my grandfather's family was full of fjord fishermen, and my great-grandfather was a shipwright in Esbjerg. I have no doubts about my refrain: *Überläufer*.

After the wake and the booze-laced coffee, I walked through Sønderho and out toward the southern tip. It was September, the sky was high, and I pressed on across the flats. I walked in the direction of Gallows Deep, talking to Johanne. I don't know if she died at a falling tide, but I know she had the Wadden Sea so deep down inside her soul that she couldn't possibly be anywhere but here. And so I stood, listening to the silence some way out, the stringed instrument. Ribe Cathedral a vast omen to the east. Feeling the vault close below me and above, I crouched down. I took a handful of wet sand and let it wring out through my fingers. The Wadden Sea is a living being with a big, damp lung.

"For the men we couldn't count on after all, Johanne. And for the tenderness we felt for them anyway," I whispered, leaving my handprint in the mud. I could have sat there for a while and seen it erased by the tide. But the tide comes in quickly in these parts, and we must gather, scatter. Welcome and goodbye. ✦

INSIDE THE HOUSE

Nicole Claveloux

Translated from the FRENCH by DONALD NICHOLSON-SMITH
LETTERING BY Dean Sudarsky

DRIP
Ama Asantewa Diaka
ILLUSTRATION BY Nicole Rifkin

"I DEY SWERVE traffic small," the bus driver says, veering off the main road. We pass a KVIP, and the unmistakable scent of collective shit rises like smoke. The houses we drive past have rusty roofs and windows with missing louvers and fading blue walls that look like water seeped into a painter's drawing.

As we reach the end of the street, a low guttural voice behind me starts humming a Presbyterian hymn. It's the one my grandmother always sings.

The woman who sits two seats ahead of me wears a navy-blue T-shirt that reads CARO MADE ME DO IT. She looks as if she is thinking about something important, with her partly squinted eyes and folded lips. I wonder if she has ever touched herself before. I wonder if she has ever touched herself in the back seat of an empty car. I wonder if the act of touching yourself in open spaces constitutes waywardness, or something completely abominable.

Once, in the bathroom of a four-star hotel, Naana and I spent thirty-two minutes trying to draw on perfect eyebrows. We had been friends for four years. I first saw her at a Spiritual Union camp. She was telling a boy he couldn't laugh at a girl for being an A cup when he had the smallest feet. We bonded instantly. We liked the same movies and were both mean to boys. We'd written and directed a one-minute short film titled "Girls on Snapchat Be Like . . ." And she'd once walked closely behind me from the mall to get a taxi just so nobody else could see the bloodstain on my skirt.

"How often do you masturbate?" She dabbed the tip of her left eyebrow with her pinkie.

I blinked and looked at her for a second too long. Her question threw me off guard. I swallowed hard and shifted uncomfortably.

"Um, I don't masturbate."

"What? Are you serious?"

"Yeah . . ."

"Ah Ayeley you're joking. Not even dry humping? Sweet baby Jesus!"

She placed the brown eye pencil on the marble sink and turned to me.

"Listen to me. Touch yourself. Touch yourself, you hear? How do you give someone permission to travel a road you've not used yourself? How do you expect the trip to be smooth when you don't know how to get there? Do not let another man visit the Promised Land when you haven't graced the walls of the land with your holiness."

A teenager with breasts three times bigger than mine blocks my view out the bus window. I remember myself as a teenager, with no breasts, figuring out life for myself, and I think this teenager will be just fine. She's wearing a red faux leather skirt that exposes a creamy thigh with two beauty spots lined up on it, as if God placed them there as an afterthought. Tiny beads of sweat cover her nose. She's gesturing wildly and telling someone on the phone that a boy called Kpakpo is a big fat liar because she, Akwele, has never read Mills & Boons or any sex novels, she reads only correct books and has even started reading John Grisham. When she says the word *sex*, it feels to me like popping a toffee into your mouth. She looks sixteen or seventeen, with large eyes and a big lower lip, and I still think she will do just fine.

✦

When I was in class 3, my teacher, Mr. Akwetey, shuffled the class and arranged the seating order such that no two boys or girls were sitting close to each other, every girl had to sit next to a boy and vice versa. That's how Larry with the big head and lazy eyes became my sitting partner. During writing class, he took my hand underneath the table and guided it to his genitals. Mr. Akwetey was painstakingly writing out *the quick brown fox jumps over the lazy dog* in cursive on the blackboard. I looked up to see if anybody could see what was happening. I looked back at Larry. He turned his attention to the blackboard and kept his hold on my wrist, moving my hand to and fro around his genitals. I felt frozen; I did not whisk my hand away. And then he pulled my skirt a little farther up and urgently pushed his fingers through. After class I stayed in my seat and refused to go for lunch even though I was dying for a strawberry lollipop. I hid my hand in my pocket and didn't take it out till my father picked me up from school.

I changed my seat the next day. Mr Akwetey made me kneel for an hour for taking Baafi's seat, but I sat in Baafi's seat for the next three days until Mr. Akwetey finally gave up. I would think often about this incident and be filled with crippling guilt. I wondered if I was a good child, and if I was, had this one sin revoked my goodness? Should I have taken my hand off? Did staying still imply my willingness? Was there anything I did to invite him to touch me that day? Did I subconsciously want to touch him? Should I have told someone about this?

The next year, my father was transferred to a church outside of the city so we moved, and I never saw Larry again.

✦

A strong smell hits my nose and I glance accusingly at the man sitting beside me. If you want to fart in an enclosed space then you can buy your own car and fart every ten minutes. I am glad to get off at the next stop.

Taking my clothes off when I get home is a hurried ritual, as if my sanity depends on how fast I can unhook my bra. The mirror repeats every action back to me and when I look myself straight in the eye, I think that it is fair to say that me, too, I be fine girl. Ink dey for my body small. My hair is impractically tough but somehow I'm able to tame it. Clothes fall easily on my side with no hips to distract them. I have had lovers tell me they love me even though I have no breasts, as though I should be thankful. I have had them explore my body with their fingers as though they were digging for a treasure just beneath the surface.

The teenager on the bus will do just fine when she learns what comes after a body is developed. When desire rents space in your body. When lust tiptoes in on random Sunday afternoons. When she discovers the urge to lie with a man who has only fleeting feelings for her. All the phone calls she has made, and the "correct" books she has read, will be pushed aside and forgotten. They will make no difference to the men she will come to love, who will then come to leave her.

I remember Madam Rita from Sunday school telling us that masturbation is a sin. I remember Pastor Michael, stiff-necked and wide-eyed, telling us how masturbation done alone and accompanied by lust is a grave sin. I remember Fred telling a group of girls that God is deeply sad whenever we go against his word and give in to the flesh, and I wonder how anybody could feel that way when there is an urgent thread of desire pushing itself out of a body, when pleasure is bonding with relief and hugging itself around my toes. I remember Auntie Jasmine threatening to tell Mommy when she saw me with my hand in my crotch on the couch after school.

I remember how as a young woman I'd slide my fingers down, imitating an ardent lover, imagining a wanton partner, the buzz and eagerness to please, the careless affection.

I slide my underwear out of the way and rock my finger to and fro. And then as the intensity builds up, as the seemingly long spurt of excitement announces itself, as it ushers in its promise of glorious release, I part my chapped lips, only ever so slightly, swallowing quick and hard, and I think of how alive this makes me feel—and then I let it drip.✦

From "WITHOUT WHICH"
Solmaz Sharif

]]

I have long loved what one can carry.
I have long left all that can be left
behind in the burning cities and lost

even loss—not cared much
or learned to. I turned and looked
and not even salt did I become.

]]

]]

I have long not wanted much
touch to turn away from and sleep
a sleep to bring the spoon up
and slurp the soup I don't notice gone.

Like that mostly, my life.

     ]]

Until I see something new.

It does not happen much.

Except in the sense that everything is new.

     ]]

Three baby teeth in a washed-clean, baby-food jar
rattling

as the drawer opens and closes or

the train passes underneath
or our bed bumps into the nightstand,

     ]]

into the wall,
sliding across the room,

chattering loose teeth I wanted to hold on to
in a glass jar for what? for how long?

Eventually I pare down

]]

what of me I can't stand to look at,

what of me I'd never want recognized,

by whoever will clear out my drawers,
whoever does such a thing at the end
of a life,

]]

who years wanted nothing,

who was dead before she died.

]]

]]

]]

]]

Before you came, I hadn't touched another
in years. It was unintentional.
Frugal.

Later and the satisfaction of a small life

closed in a single mind.

      ]]

Your thin drawer.

Pocket squares folded into neat stacks.
Wristwatches laid flat into neat–

You looked at me
looking at your things.

      ]]

I touched the satin squares.

I touched the satin scar
where you had been cut.

      ]]

Your healthy walking.
Your wristwatch removed

and ticking in this room.
To watch you
get dressed while still in bed

]]

is a little city where
I'm most grateful to be alive, gently

ticking—naked, leisurely
watching a slightly warped record

turn, its tiny hills

]]

raising the needle, too, gently.

]]

WIST

Mieko Kawakami

Translated from the JAPANESE by HITOMI YOSHIO

ERIA

THE WORKERS CAME and destroyed the outer walls. The brick wall fell apart like a cake demolished at random by a child with a fork. The next day, the garden was revealed.

The wisteria tree, the one whose flowers bloomed behind the walls every spring, could be seen in its totality. Its dark trunk seemed thicker than the branches had suggested, and next to its roots was a pond in the shape of a gourd. The water had already been drained, and old, colorless leaves covered the bottom. Behind the pond was an old-fashioned porch. When the small yellow excavator came the following day, it made a low, angry growl and started digging up the garden.

It took only thirty minutes to cut down the wisteria tree. Its roots, abandoned on the dirt, resembled arms that grasped at something in midair. The excavator crushed everything, mixing the laundry pole, the flowerpots, and the stones. It trampled the porch and bulldozed through the house, mercilessly clawing through the furniture and screen doors. *So that's how you destroy a house*, I thought, half-amused and impressed. The old two-story house that had stood majestically in the corner lot diagonally across the road was being destroyed, and I was watching the spectacle from my second-floor kitchen window.

An old woman had lived there. I would sometimes see her. When we moved into the neighborhood six years ago, we tried to pay a visit to the house a few times, but no one ever answered the door. Every once in a while, I would pass the old woman on the street as she walked slowly around the house in the morning and evening hours, leaning against a cart. We never exchanged greetings, and yet I felt strangely serene in those moments. She always wore a black blouse with a black cardigan draped over her shoulders, and in the spring evenings, I would see her walking slowly out of the rusted gate onto the sidewalk with a broom and dustpan in her hands. When the wisteria tree shed its flowers, the gray asphalt would be covered in shades of white and pale purple, and every time the wind blew, the petals would dance in the air. The old woman would spend a long time sweeping up those petals from one corner of the road to the other. The petals fell even on seemingly windless nights, and the following day, the old woman would emerge slowly with her broom and dustpan again. This would continue until the flowers were gone. But I had not seen her recently. When was the last time I saw her?

"I wonder if that old woman passed away," I mentioned during dinner one night.

After a pause, my husband grumbled something inaudible, his eyes still fixed to the TV screen.

"They're doing work over there. It's been so noisy."

"Hmm. Looks like they're demolishing the house," he said.

I stacked my own dinner plates and took them over to the kitchen sink. I watched as my husband nibbled on his vegetable stir-fry while sipping a can of beer, laughing soundlessly at the TV.

It had been nine years since I married my husband, who was three years older. I had been twenty-nine at the time, and he had been thirty-two.

Three years after the wedding, we bought this house. My husband had a job in the sales department at an international pharmaceutical company, and every morning, he left for work at eight o'clock. After seeing him off, I would sweep around the house and water the grounds, put the towels and sheets in the laundry machine and press the start button. I would vacuum the living room and the other two rooms. At eleven thirty, I would eat a simple lunch, then walk to the supermarket near the station to buy groceries. My husband hated the fridge being full, so I went to the supermarket every day to buy only the things I needed that day. Our fridge was always empty.

I would scrub the kitchen methodically and wipe down the windows. Around six, I would make dinner and eat on my own. I would turn on the TV, then I would turn off the TV. Around ten, my husband would come home. I would heat up his dinner while he took a shower. My husband sometimes told lies. He would watch late-night TV shows while sipping beer and eating, then crawl into bed and stare at the pale screen on his smartphone for a long time. Every morning, my husband would wake up with dark circles around his eyes. He would slump his body against the door and leave the house.

We started considering having children around the time we bought the house, and for a while we tried. But I didn't get pregnant—which was a possibility I had never considered. With no preexisting condition and regular periods, I had assumed that it was all a matter of timing. But six months passed since I had begun taking my daily temperature, then a year, and still nothing happened.

After some online research, I realized that we were already at a stage when we needed to begin treatment at a specialized clinic. For two months, I buried myself in books about fertility treatments in the library and scoured the internet. I felt a wave of anxiety that my body had perhaps already lost the ability to conceive. One thing was for certain—if I wanted to get pregnant, I needed to start treatment as soon as possible. And for that, the understanding and cooperation of my husband was crucial.

One evening, I brought up the subject with my husband. I suggested that we go to a clinic together to find out why we weren't getting pregnant, and that both of us needed to be examined. I chose my words carefully and explained as best I could.

My husband was clipping his toenails. Looking up, he furrowed his eyebrows and made a disgusted expression. That expression. It felt as if I were being stabbed with something sharp between my lungs every time.

"What do you mean, *examined*? It's not like you're sick, are you?"

"It's not about being sick," I answered carefully. "My period comes regularly, but it doesn't mean I'm ovulating. And even if I were, I still need to make sure the eggs are functioning properly."

"We need to go together," I continued without looking his way. "We've been trying for a year now and nothing has happened, so there must be some reason . . . We won't know what the problem is until we're both properly examined."

My husband threw the clipped nails into the trash can. Then he stared off into space at the white wall. After some time, his cell phone began to ring. "It's my business partner . . ." he muttered under his breath and left the living room to go downstairs. I heard him say hello as the door closed behind him.

He brought up the subject again one night, two weeks later, after the bedroom lights had been turned off. "About that clinic you were talking about . . . I think we should just let things take their course."

I remained silent.

"They say children are a blessing—not something you force. And there's no end to fertility treatments once you start. People spend ten million yen and still get nowhere. Plus, it's not like we desperately wanted one, right?"

My husband's voice assaulted me in the darkness, coming at me like the index finger of a relentless auditor that scrutinizes product defects. I kept my eyes open in the dark, thinking about the pain in my chest. After a while, he seemed to have fallen asleep.

From that day on, we never talked about having children again, and my husband stopped initiating sex. Before long, I was thirty-eight and my husband was forty-one.

✦

It was during the last week of March that I noticed the sound had stopped. I had assumed the demolition work was put on hold due to rain, but come to think of it, there hadn't been any rain in a while. Looking through the kitchen window, I could see the house still in the process of demolition, only about a third of the way through. When had they stopped?

I listened but there was no sound. It was so quiet. What did people around here do this time of day? Who on earth were these "people" anyway? Even the next-door neighbors were strangers—I knew nothing about them aside from their general family compositions and the colors of their cars. After observing the house for a while, I went down the stairs, put on my sneakers, and went outside.

Although it was only March, the sun beat down and made me sweat under my thin sweater. The house lay exposed and immobile beyond the rubble. I had passed by countless times since the demolition began, but this was the first time I stopped to examine the house carefully. It looked much larger than it had from my second-floor kitchen window.

Pieces of broken debris gleamed sharply in the sun, and the paint can that the workers had used as an ashtray was buried halfway in the dirt. A heavy shovel lay abandoned on the ground. A glove was stuck to a wooden plank, and glimmering shards of glass mingled with the dirt and debris. Dry white mud caked the caterpillar track of the excavator, its scoop still filled with dirt as if it had lost its way in midair.

I must have been gazing at the house for five or ten minutes when I felt a presence and looked up. There was a woman standing on the left-hand side of the property, where the gate and entrance used to be. She was about my height and wore a long-sleeve black dress. Her arms, which hung by her side, seemed disproportionately long. She was staring at the house, just like I was.

"No sign of rain," the woman said. Then she slowly made her way over to me until we were standing side by side. She seemed to be around my age. Her face, with no trace of makeup, was covered in spots, and her forehead seemed shockingly narrow against her thick black hair, which was tied back. Her hands were empty.

"I've been coming here since they started the demolition," she said.

"I live just over there," I said, pointing to my house.

"Doesn't the noise bother you?"

"Not too much," I responded.

"I wouldn't be able to stand it. You know, that peculiar sound."

"Peculiar sound?"

The woman nodded, her face still turned to the house. "The sound of something being destroyed."

The sound of something being destroyed . . . I gazed at the house before me but couldn't recall any particular sound from the past few weeks.

"But aren't there all kinds of sounds?" I asked. "Depending on the material. . ."

"Material?"

"Yes, well . . . glass would make a different sound from wood, right?"

"That's not what I'm talking about. Whatever the material or size, there's a kind of *essence* of sound that can be heard only when something is being destroyed. It's like catching a single note within a chord. I can hear it mixed with other sounds. You can detect a sort of intention."

"Intention?"

"I'm not sure if it's the intention of the destroyer or the destroyed, but I can hear it. It makes a world of difference whether something is destroyed naturally or by external force."

I had difficulty comprehending what the woman was trying to say. As I searched for words, she took a step into the property and began walking toward the house.

"I've never been here during the day," the woman said after some time.

"During the day?"

"I usually go into empty properties at night."

"Empty properties?" I echoed with surprise. "What do you mean?"

"An apartment, a condo, a house. It doesn't matter what kind, just as long as it's empty."

"Why at night? So you don't get caught?"

"There's that. But I really like houses at night."

I thought to myself, *It must be so dark* . . .

"Of course," she said, as if she had read my mind, "the circuit breaker is switched off, so it's pitch dark. I enter the darkness and sit in the living room, or in the center of the room if it's a studio. Then I lie down and open and close my eyes slowly. The eyes adjust after a while, and you start to see all kinds of things. Light finds its way in even at night, no matter how small the window may be."

I imagined the woman opening and closing her eyes in the dark.

"Yes, like that. I lie in the room for a while. Then, I leave."

"What about the keys? How do you find these empty properties in the first place?"

"Real estate agent websites. I look through their rentals. Expensive properties are no good since they tend to have tight security. Same with upscale condos with a front desk. Old buildings are best, especially if the apartment has been sitting for a month or two since the listing. You can usually find the keys taped to the top of the mailbox, or attached to the side of the pipe closet or the meter box. Or they could be sitting on top of the gas meter. If I can't find the keys, I just give up. One in three, I find a way in."

I tried to imagine an abandoned house in the middle of the night. No furniture, no human breath, just darkness alone. Then, light finds its way through the windows, eroding the room in shades of blue. A woman's arms, plump with blue shadow, slowly extend toward me. I looked up. The woman was still gazing at the house.

"Did you go inside this one?"

The woman shook her head. "I came as soon as I heard about the estate sale, but the demolition work had already started. It's not every day you come across such a large house, so I was quite disappointed."

We fell silent and gazed at the house together.

The woman with the long arms looked up. "Smells like rain," she said.

*

From that evening, it rained for two days straight.

I vacuumed every corner of the house with more care than usual and scrubbed the floors with a tightly wrung towel. The rain turned into a downpour, and the wind blew against the windows so hard it seemed like someone was running across them. I listened to the low tremor of thunder in the distance.

My husband came home late. "I'm entertaining clients this weekend," he grumbled while watching TV. His boss had come down with a stomach flu, so he would have to take them golfing instead. It would be an overnight trip. "We're going to the hot springs and it's not even winter," he complained. I listened half-heartedly while doing the dishes, then leaned against the cupboard and looked out the window. Beyond my own face reflected on the dark murky window, the house stood in the depth of the night.

The darkness, the desolate sound of the winds, the low growl of thunder, the unceasing rain—everything seemed to flow out of the house like a wound, half-destroyed and laid bare. The rainwater came alive as it made its way down the gentle slope below. I pressed my fingers on the glass as if to touch the movement—then noticed my husband's voice.

"Are you listening?"

"Sorry," I said. I hadn't heard a word he said.

Early Saturday morning, my husband loaded his golf bag in the car trunk and drove off. I finished the housework as usual and waited for night to come. Three days had passed since the torrential rain. The sun moved slowly across the sky, and as the dusk melted into asphalt and trees and houses, darkness fell. A dog barked. A young woman talked into her cell phone. A motorcycle drove by, its engine blasting. Then the sounds ceased. At one o'clock in the morning, I left the house.

Small puddles remained in what was once the garden. My whole body felt stiff, and I could feel my back starting to sweat. I advanced little by little, holding my breath. The closer I got, the farther the house seemed to move away from me. When I looked back, I saw a faint round light. It took a while for me to realize that it was the entryway light to my own house.

The tatami mat was dry, thanks to the half-remaining roof. I took off my sneakers with some hesitation and placed them inside what must have been the living room, now half-destroyed, and proceeded to go farther on my hands and knees. When I came to a pillar, I stood up and passed the alcove I had seen from afar, then continued to tread with caution toward the right-hand side.

It did not take long for the shapes to appear on the tatami mat, like a hidden pattern in a trompe l'œil picture. Worn pencil with the eraser still attached. White coffee cup. Large wall calendar covered in cloth, caked with mud. Magazines with pages falling out. Grand prize shield with gold plates. A cord, perhaps. An entire drawer overflowing with sheets of bundled paper. And then there was a set of two dark-colored sofas. Behind them were a shelf and what looked like a record player. I advanced slowly while studying these objects one by one, and eventually reached a narrow corridor that led to the interior of the house.

In the corridor, the blue light that had filled the room until a moment ago receded, and a thick darkness of an entirely different quality engulfed me. The darkness became thicker as I inched forward, and my heart began to make a drumming sound. Eventually the corridor came to an end, and my toes touched a doorsill on the left-hand side. Extending my feet, I could feel carpet. *Here's another room.* When I swallowed the saliva that had accumulated in my mouth, it made a sound so loud my body shook. I took a step into the room.

The room was filled with profound silence and darkness. I could no longer see myself. *Shouldn't I go back the way I came, crawling on all fours, to return to a place where there is light?* Suddenly overcome by fear, I felt my heart beat faster. I realized then that I had no water with me. I wetted my lips several times. My mouth felt dry. I took a deep breath, telling myself to calm down. *My house is on the other side of the street. If I get thirsty, all I need to do is go back. Everything will be all right.* But was it true? Did such a place—a home to go back to—really exist?

My eyes showed no sign of adjusting to the dark, no matter how long I stood there. The darkness seemed to exclude light altogether. And yet I kept walking farther into the room. The living room was strewn with countless objects, but this room was different. I could feel the carpet under my feet and nothing else. Taking three more steps, I lowered my body and fell to my knees. I placed my hands on the carpet and gradually moved them outward in a stroking motion, as if drawing small circles with my fingers. Still nothing. Then slowly, I leaned back and lay down. As I relaxed my limbs and lay still, the boundary between myself and the darkness became more and more ambiguous.

What kind of room was this?

I couldn't make out the color or pattern of the carpet, nor was there anything peculiar about the texture. It was impossible to tell how big the room was or how it was arranged, whether it was a Japanese-style or Western-style room. Was it a bedroom, perhaps, or a study, or a children's room? A storage room, or even a walk-in closet? I imagined the old woman with her white hair pulled back, hunched over a cart and walking slowly around the house, meticulously sweeping the fallen wisteria petals. Where did she spend most of her time in this large house?

I realized I knew nothing about the old woman, not even her name. I tried in vain to recall the name plate in front of the house. Could she have been eighty years old, or perhaps even ninety? It was hard to guess the age after a certain point. How long had she been living alone? The house seemed much too large for one person to occupy. When I tried to picture the house, however, I realized I couldn't even remember what it looked like.

What I could recall was the exterior wall, made of reddish-brown brick that you would see anywhere. Standing behind it was the wisteria tree, which had the most exquisite color. I would often gaze at the hanging flowers from my kitchen window or from the street on my way to and from the store. Next to the large rusty iron gate hung a well-worn placard for an English-language school for children. The sign was difficult to read due to rain and wind damage, but one could make out a foreign name written in large katakana letters. And beside it was a Japanese woman's name. MS. ** WILL TEACH YOU ENGLISH, the sign had stated proudly. But what was her name?

I tried to imagine the old woman as a young teacher, giving English lessons to a small group of children. Enveloped in total darkness, my imagination was strangely vivid and raw. She is in her mid-thirties. Her thick lustrous black hair pulled back, she peers into children's notebooks while resting her hands on their desks and checking for mistakes. From time to time, the foreign teacher pronounces the words in English, opening her mouth wide so the children can see the movement of her tongue. *Seals. Owl. Umbrella.* The children, having just entered primary school, repeat the English words. The foreign teacher smiles and reads aloud the next set of vocabulary. She is some years older than the old woman. Two dimples are visible on her red cheeks against her pale skin. Her hair, so blond that it looks white depending on the light, is cut short, and she towers over the petite old woman by at least half a foot. Whenever they were in the classroom, the two women always wore black blouses in various types of fabric. They never made a conscious decision to do so, but it became a kind of unspoken agreement.

The foreign teacher arrives at ten o'clock in the morning. Over a hot cup of tea, the two women go over the lesson plans for the day, followed by lunch at the kitchen table. Sometimes the old woman would make thin wheat noodles, and other times the foreign teacher would bring simple sandwiches. After clearing away the dishes, the foreign teacher would listen to a record in the living room. On that particular day, she brings over her favorite record and invites the old woman to listen as she carefully places it on the turntable and drops the needle. They sit side by side on the small velvet sofas and listen. Piano Sonata no. 32, second movement—Beethoven's final piano sonata. The old woman closes her eyes. Listening to the soft and soothing voice of the foreign teacher as she talks about the piece and the female pianist performing it, the old woman experiences an inexplicable feeling, at once dark and happy, like an endlessly spreading gray sky. Over the years, they would listen to the piece over and over, more times than they could count.

The children are generally quiet during lessons, writing neatly in their notebooks with their pencils. Aside from the girl sitting by the window who has a habit of letting her eyes wander, the students are well behaved for the most part and listen attentively to the teachers. The classroom is on the upper floor of the house in a large Western-style room with a wooden floor, and different students occupy the room depending on the time and day of the week. Saturday afternoons were reserved for upper primary school children.

Does one of the children belong to the old woman? Probably not. Since her father passed away about ten years ago, she has lived in this house alone. She was brought up by her father, in this house that had escaped war damage, and aside from the absence of her mother, she lived a privileged life and received an excellent education. She never married. Her father's efforts in matchmaking were in vain. The old woman loved the English language, and by the time she was fifteen years old, she could read simple novels in English. In college, she studied modern British literature and fell in love with Virginia Woolf. Clutching her dictionary, she would try to decipher Woolf's complex sentences, which seemed to weave together a beautiful tapestry with shadows falling here and there, never repeating the same pattern twice.

One day, the old woman met the foreign teacher in a small reading group. The foreign teacher told her all kinds of stories about the town of Chelmsford, where she grew up. She also told her about London—about the air raids, Westminster Cathedral, the fountain of St. James's Park and how the light would dance on the water, the coronation ceremony of Queen Elizabeth II, the curse of London Bridge. It didn't take long for the two to become best friends. And one year later, the two women decided to open an English-language school together, in the house where the old woman had been living on her own since her father passed away.

The wisteria tree had stood in the garden since long before the old woman was born. Every year, the tree blossoms with flowers, gently swelling into pale pink and purple clusters as if inhaling the dreams of dawn. In springtime, the two women would sit side by side on the porch between classes and look up at the tree. "Wisteria," the foreign teacher would sometimes murmur, as if filling the blank space between herself and the flowers. That day, as they sit gazing at the wisteria tree side by side like always, the foreign teacher suddenly asks the old woman if she could call her Wisteria.

"Sure. But why?"

"Everyone has a real name. I can guess what it is. After knowing someone for a while, I start seeing the name appear in the middle of their face. I figured out soon after I met you that your name was Wisteria."

Wisteria, the old woman whispers in her mind. *Wisteria*. The name, with such a foreign ring, tickles her and makes her blush. She tries saying it aloud. "Wisteria."

At the foot of the wisteria tree is a pond shaped like a gourd, with a few medium-size carp swimming in it. The pond shimmers every time the wind blows, and if one watches the movement of the water, it seems possible to touch a soft part of some distant forgotten memory. On especially windy days, the petals would fall and cover the water in white, and the two women would scoop them up endlessly with their nets.

One spring afternoon, the third spring since they started their English-language school, the foreign teacher loses her balance on the edge stone and falls into the pond, taking along Wisteria, who instinctively grabs her hand. Seeing each other sitting in the pond, the two women burst out laughing. Clothes soaking wet and covered with petals, water dropping from the tips of their hair, softly shining in the light. Seeing the foreign teacher laugh makes Wisteria laugh, but after a while she becomes aware of emotions she has never known before. It isn't pain or aching or sorrow exactly—whatever it is, that shadow engulfs her and makes her look away from the brilliance before her.

The two women would finish their work around seven o'clock in the evening. Then, it would be time for the foreign teacher to leave. Sometimes they would have dinner together at the house, and other times, they would walk down to a soba shop near the station. No matter how late it is, the foreign teacher never stays the night. The two always wave goodbye at the entrance of the house or by the train station.

From the living room, Wisteria would walk through the corridor to reach her bedroom. Unlike the sunlit living room and garden which faced south, the north-facing bedroom seems to exist in a perpetual bluish shadow, remaining cool even at the height of summer. The nights are especially long. Turning off the light, Wisteria would lie on her back in the darkness and breathe in and out. "Drop upon drop, silence falls . . . As silence falls I am dissolved utterly and become featureless and scarcely to be distinguished from another." Wisteria stares at the words that suddenly came to her, blinking in the darkness. Ah . . . it was Woolf. The waves rushing to the shore, eternally, yet never to return. "In this silence . . . it seems as if no leaf would ever fall, or bird fly." The characters whisper. " As if the miracle had happened."

Wisteria imagines the doorbell ringing—with the force of a prayer, she imagines it ringing. She rushes out of her bedroom and heads for the entrance. When she opens the door, the foreign teacher is standing there. "I left something behind," she says with a shy smile. Wisteria takes her hand and invites her inside. She is on the verge of tears, overcome by the feeling of ecstasy upon touching her beloved's body for the first time. In silence, the two join their bodies together. Wisteria slowly extends her arms. Holding her breath, she stretches her arms straight before her. But the only things her fingers touch are the cold lonely particles of darkness that fill the room, where she lies all alone.

There is no doorbell. There is no miracle.

The days pass uneventfully. Wisteria is not released from her nightly suffering. She lies on her back in the bedroom, her hands placed on her stomach, waiting for sleep to take her away from the here and now. But she is wide awake.

In the darkness, Wisteria clenches her hands, which rest on her stomach. She closes her eyes, then opens them again. *I never gave birth*. At thirty-eight, it is the first time that she puts the thought into words. She finds the thought almost comical, after all this time. She has never touched a man, even held hands, never felt any romantic feeling whatsoever. It seems humorous somehow that someone who has never desired nor been desired would think of such a thing as that.

But that evening, the thought of a child captures Wisteria's imagination and does not release her. *What does it mean to give birth? How does it feel to have a baby grow inside your body?* Staring into the dark with these thoughts, Wisteria begins to hear a faint cry coming from somewhere. It is a baby crying—Wisteria is sitting on a sunny porch, cradling a tiny baby in her arms. The baby has the same color hair as the foreign teacher, so blond that it looks almost white in the sun. Wisteria knows instantly that this baby, clasping its tiny wrinkled hands next to its mouth, belongs to her and the foreign teacher. How or where the baby came from, she doesn't know. But she knows it is their baby girl. A feeling of love rushes forth from within. *Our daughter*. Wisteria gazes and gazes at the face of the sleeping baby, places her gently in the basket so as not to wake her, and closes her own eyes to succumb to a warm afternoon slumber. When Wisteria awakens, the baby is gone. Inside the basket, only the blanket remains with the baby's imprint. She screams. She realizes, then, that she is lying on her back in a profound darkness that was even deeper than before.

Her heart beats fast. The tears crawl around her temples to the back of her head like a living thread. They wrap around her neck and strangle her. In the darkness, Wisteria tells herself, *The baby doesn't exist. Nowhere in this world does the baby exist. There's no such thing as our baby. Even if we were to act on our love—though it would never happen—we still could not have a baby girl together. Because I am a woman, and she is a woman.*

One day, the foreign teacher departs. Her mother has fallen ill, and she needs to return to England to take care of her. "I love this country. I love our work together. I'll be back as soon as things are settled. In the meantime, I can introduce you to someone who can teach the children on my behalf." Wisteria shakes her head and says she'll try to manage on her own. It is the tenth spring since they opened the English-language school together. The wisteria tree has flowered beautifully this year, as always. The two women sit side by side on the porch, watching the petals fall one by one on the surface of the pond and on the warm soil of the garden.

"Do they have wisteria trees in England?"

"Of course. Lots of them," the foreign teacher answers.

In silence, they gaze at the wisteria flowers together. Then, after some time, the foreign teacher says, "I had a child once." Wisteria looks at her face as if struck by lightning. The foreign teacher keeps her eyes on the wisteria tree and continues in a low voice.

"I don't have one anymore. The baby died. It was a long time ago, almost thirty years. The baby lived for only three months." She exhales and looks over at Wisteria's face for the first time, smiling faintly.

The foreign teacher leaves for England. Wisteria receives letters from her twice a month, which becomes once every two months, then once every six months, then eventually a Christmas card once a year. Perhaps that was all to be expected. They were close friends who trusted each other and worked together for a decade, but they had never made any future promises to each other.

One day, after the same number of years had passed as they had spent together, Wisteria sits down and writes a letter with singular hope. Although the two have grown apart, Wisteria wishes to see the foreign teacher again even just once. It is unlikely that she would return to Japan. So why not travel to England herself? Wisteria has never traveled abroad in her life, but if the foreign teacher were to reply with the words, *It's been so long. How are you? It would be lovely to see you again*, then she feels she could do anything. Wisteria worries about how much she has aged, being already near seventy, but more than that, she is moved by the strong desire to see the foreign teacher again. She spends many days writing the letter.

But no reply comes. Wisteria waits a month, then six months. She does not receive a Christmas card that year. Had she written something to offend her? Or was the letter itself unwelcome? Wisteria thinks of all the possibilities, but there is no way to find out the truth. Wisteria spends the winter full of anxiety and depression, but as winter gives way to the fragrance of spring, filling the air, a letter arrives. One afternoon, Wisteria sits on the porch amid the falling petals and reads the letter from England. It contains news of the foreign teacher's death. "I was her colleague," the letter explains. "She had lung cancer, and by the time she was diagnosed, it was too late. She died within three months. This past spring. There was a will, but it contained mostly administrative matters. There was no mention of you. I'm writing to you of my own accord because I found a stack of letters from you when I was organizing her belongings. I thought it best to let you know. Please don't take it hard. She went to heaven without suffering."

Wisteria closes the English-language school and begins spending her days alone in the house. She wakes up in the morning, gets dressed, and spends a long time cleaning the house. She goes to the kitchen and scrubs all her unused pots and plates and wipes down the inside of the empty refrigerator. Before dust has a chance to settle, she dusts all of the furniture and sweeps the tatami mats. She keeps sweeping the invisible dust with a broom as if caressing the traces of time that has passed.

That was when Wisteria was still able-bodied. After a while, her consciousness begins to shift shape and change color, and her body becomes so weak that she can no longer leave the bedroom. Darkness torments her without mercy. That day the letter arrived replays endlessly in her mind. It is spring. As wisteria petals scatter like snow in the wind, Wisteria learns the news of the foreign teacher's death. A single image whispers its presence to her once again, one that had visited her repeatedly since the foreign teacher left. It is the baby—dead three months after it was born. *It's all my fault.* Wisteria opens her eyes in the dark. *The baby died because I wished for a baby together and held it in my arms.*

It is illogical, of course. The foreign teacher's baby had died long before they ever met, and time would have to be reversed for the two events to connect. But Wisteria understands. She had felt emotions she was forbidden to have, desired what was not meant to be desired. She had caressed the baby's fair hair, which did not exist, and brought her face to its soft cheeks and inhaled its gentle breath. And for that, the baby was lost. *Please don't take it hard. She went to heaven without suffering.* The wind blows. It is as if all the winds in the world come gushing toward Wisteria. The wisteria tree shakes, and the petals turn into a whirlpool that engulfs her. She cannot see. She cannot breathe. In the darkness, resting her withered hands on her chest, Wisteria thinks these thoughts as she takes her final breath.

I have been here from the beginning. I have been here all along.

　✦

I opened my eyes and blinked several times. I slowly exhaled the air that remained in my chest, then breathed in again deeply. My body felt heavy, and I could barely move my limbs. My head throbbed. There was a piercing pain in my hips. I had no idea how long I had been lying there. My body ached with a distinct sensation that signaled an oncoming fever. A chill ran down my back, and my breath felt hot.

My mind, on the other hand, felt eerily acute. When I opened my mouth, my back teeth stuttered. It was cold. My entire body ached with grating pain. As I sat up slowly on the carpet and rubbed my shoulders, I came upon a realization. The texture of the darkness had changed.

Ever since I entered, the room had been filled with an impenetrable darkness. I had become part of that darkness and the darkness had become part of me. But now it was different. The darkness had transformed into a bluish shadow that gently illuminated my arms and thighs and feet.

Light finds its way in even at night, no matter how small the window may be. It was just as she had said.

I don't remember how I left the house, walked across the muddy grounds littered with debris, and arrived home. Countless large raindrops pelted my body. I took off my sneakers by the door, went up the stairs straight into the kitchen without turning on the light, pulled a glass out of the cupboard, and drank two glassfuls of water from the tap. I grabbed a towel and wiped my face and hair, which were both dripping wet. My body wouldn't stop shaking.

"Where were you? Do you know what time it is?"

There was a dark, sunken figure on the sofa in the living room. It was my husband.

Resting my weight against the sink, I stared at my husband's shadow floating in the dark. *Why is he here?* But I no longer cared. He floated there in the darkness like an obscure lump of shadow. Looking at the lump, I realized I could no longer remember his face. *Who is this man?*

"Can't you answer me?"

I could sense him standing up and saw a shadow moving slowly to the door. In the next moment, the light was switched on. The kitchen and living room suddenly became flooded with light, and I flinched and instinctively shut my eyes tight.

"What's going on?"

The voice I heard in the distance seemed to be trembling, and I looked up and peered through my eyelids. Because my eyes had been closed for so long, my vision was muddled and it took a while to form a clear image. My husband was staring at me.

"What is that?"

I followed my husband's gaze and looked down.

My body, soaked in rain, was covered in white.

From my arms and chest, stomach and thighs, to calves and ankles, countless white things covered my body like fish scales. They were wisteria petals. The petals, still tinged with color, were soft and moist and looked as if they had just left the branch. They clung to my body, still alive. They even fell even on my neck and shoulders.

"What the hell happened?"

I looked straight into my husband's face. So this is what the man looked like. Why didn't I realize until now?

"Who are you?" my husband continued in a nervous voice that seemed to trail off.

"I don't know," I said. "All I know is that it has nothing to do with you."

The raindrops pelted the outer walls and windows more intensely than before. The strong wind swayed the branches and rustled the leaves. Eventually, I noticed something else mixed in with the sounds. It was a sound so faint that if I didn't listen carefully, it would be lost. But the sound pursued me. The sound came straight at me and sought me to listen. From the crevice of the rubble, from the fragments of broken glass, from the rifts of the demolished tree, from the unearthed dirt—from within myself. ✦

THREE YARDS
Jos Charles

sunset beach

Coughing through weather bees won't stop following me in, I stained my shirt, trying
to remove a stain from my shirt.

I tied my leg, how
could it be otherwise, to yours.

I laid the blanket down.

I'd stand, no swimmer am I, before the horns, two of them, in the waves.

Come back from the dead,
I bow between your hands.

Come back
from the dead, I bow between your hands.

Forgive me, I am a painter, I do not understand landscapes, I paint them.

a grave

At the gate, enmasked, jar of eucalyptus and sunflower in my hand—

it is never too early
to start planning—the grounds
keeper says, handing me his card.

(I had kept, for years, my eyes fixed on floors, trembling, *look up*, you'd said, & when I did—
branches, windowframes,
whole air-conditioning units in them).

Beside a birchling, low,
bending, *yes*, he says,
found it—

a patch
of yellow

not yet marked with name.

The sun fell low so the hour had something to name.

55

From the floor you and I sit, we see two crows caw in a nearby tree.

The one among the twigs.
The one catching sun.
The one, iridescent, wordless, backside of comb.
The one midworld in the wind.
The one with what fits in her belly.
The one with what fits in her belly.
The one solitary above a wave.
The one, *draw it*, she says, *before it's gone.*
The one with her wand.
And the one she drew.
And the one she knows.
And the one she loves.
And the one she knew.

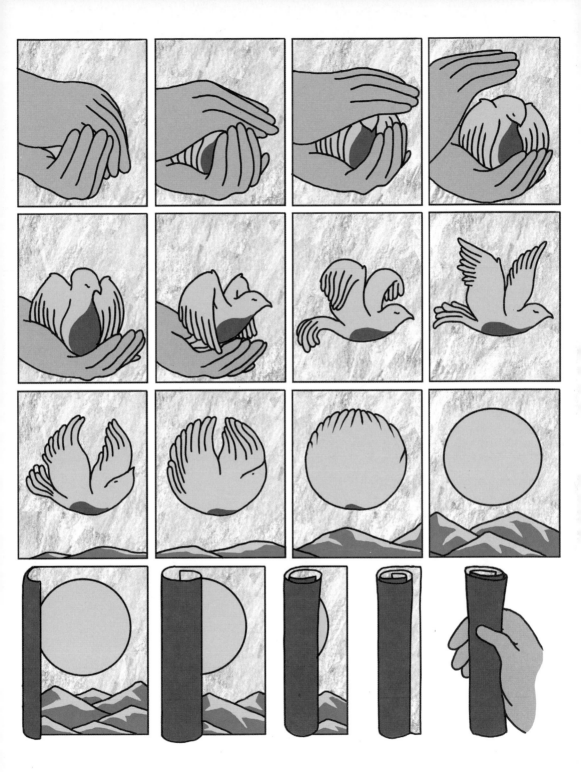

Evan M. Cohen

A
LAMB
HIMSELF
Ottessa Moshfegh

THE FLOWERS WERE still shy and wistful, their buds just breaking into bloom as it was early spring yet. There were bloodred poppies growing alongside the road, and Jude picked some as Villiam's guards passed, marching in tandem toward the village. Jude pretended they didn't exist. He didn't like northerners. He thought they carried an element of evil. Their light hair never seemed dirty, and their skin never showed any signs of wear. He didn't trust men so clean. They understood only the surfaces of things, which was why they appeared so perfect. They took Jude's depth and pain as weakness, he thought. They didn't respect his thoughtfulness. They saw him and his son as farm animals, no better than the lambs he and his son raised. And they seemed not to care about the villagers' safety. Not once during an attack by bandits had the guards defended the village. They retreated up the mountain to the manor and took aim. That was all. They were cowards, Jude thought. What he didn't know, of course, was that the bandits worked for Villiam. He paid them to ransack the village any time there was a rumor of dissent among the farmers. Father Barnabas conveyed such rumors to the lord. That was his primary function as the village priest: to listen to the confessions of the people down below and report any sagging dispositions or laziness to the man above. Terror and grief were good for morale, Villiam believed.

To get to Agata's grave, Jude and Marek passed into the woods. There were horse chestnuts on the ground. Swine were let to pannage there, and as Marek and Jude walked along they could hear some snorts and squeals. Past those woods was an orchard of apple trees, too old to bear fruit. The silver bark was thick as armor and laced high with the scars from years and years of villagers etching their names with X's. Past the orchard, the grass was thin, the dirt pale and rocky, but as it had just rained, the ground gave in a pleasant way under Jude's bare feet and Marek's thin-soled shoes. Marek picked a handful of chamomile and cornflowers growing near a trail of runoff, then followed an ostrich fern off the path toward a patch of iris. He picked an iris in bloom and some young sprigs of freesia. Then they turned toward a grove of black poplars, where, under the largest tree, was Agata's grave.

Marek was solemn as they walked, his stomach churning and his mind still darkened by the scene in the village square. Of course he had seen bandits hanged and disemboweled before, but there was something special about this man. He hadn't looked scared as Villiam's men dragged him to the gallows. Maybe he knew where he was going. Like Jesus on the Cross.

"That bandit," Marek said. "Do you think he had a mother?"

"Everybody's got a mother," Jude replied.

"Is that bandit's mother sorry he's dead?"

"They aren't like us. They have no hearts."

"Do you think he had a son of his own?"

"A bastard, surely, if he did. Who cares?"

"Did my mother love me?"

"She died for you," Jude said. "That should be enough."

"Will I see her in heaven?"

"Of course you will. As long as you get there."

"What about you?"

"Don't worry about me, Marek," Jude said.

But Marek did worry that his father wouldn't get into heaven. The man had an unkind hand. And when he prayed, Marek had the sense that there was anger steaming off his father's shoulders, the cruelty inside him escaping like a vapor. Not that the man was impious. But Jude's piety was a kind of violent urge and not the love and peace it ought to be, Marek thought. Jude whipped himself every Friday and had taught Marek to do the same. But Marek thought Jude whipped himself a bit too passionately. He'd get sweaty, grunting, moving the whip across one shoulder, then the other, wincing and breathing so hard that spit drooled from his mouth, and then he sucked it in and spat it out violently, as though it pleased him, as though the pain felt good. This frightened Marek because he, too, enjoyed the pain, and he was ashamed of that. Since he was little, a scraped knee or a whipped back, anything to make his body hurt, felt like the hand of God upon him. He knew that wasn't right. So he kept it private, which made his father's shameless display of pain and pleasure seem all the more perverse. All Marek really wanted at this age was to go to heaven, where God and his mother would love him.

"But what if something goes wrong?" he asked Jude. "What if you don't make it to heaven?"

"If God wills it, I will."

Agata's grave was marked with a plain, rounded rock from the stream. Jude had hammered a violent chip into the rock as though he really was broken by the girl's death. Jude was illiterate, like everyone else in Lapvona, but he said that the chip in the rock had a meaningful shape.

It was Marek's custom to lie down on his mother's grave, placing his body crosswise as though he were a babe in her dead arms through the dirt. He had always felt that the ground below him was charged with a sense of belonging. He would lie there and gaze up at the swaying branches of the poplar tree and listen for a birdsong. A bee-eater or an oriole might tweet a few happy notes. Marek would take this as his mother singing down to him from heaven. Now, standing by the grave, he heard a magpie song. It was angry and harsh, raspy chatter like an old lady scolding him from her window.

"Why don't you lie down today?" Jude asked, placing the flowers by the chipped stone.

"Not today. The birds are singing too sad a song."

Jude didn't believe in birdsong. He didn't trust birds. They weren't of the land, and he was a man of the land. He loved his lambs because they were like him. They were drawn to the comfort of the pasture, following the edge of the sun-drawn shadows to stay cool and warm according to the breeze. Jude was like that. He was a slave to the day as it rose and fell, and he felt this was his righteous duty—lamb herding was his God-given occupation. He ignored the church bells. He didn't need to track his time. Nature did it for him. He was born in that pasture and felt he would die in it, too. Why had he not buried Agata in the pasture? Marek had asked a few times. Jude would never entertain such a question.

"Let's go then," Jude said, already turning back toward the woods.

The path they'd worn from Agata's grave through the woods to the pasture was narrow because Jude and Marek never walked side by side. Jude always walked in front. Marek knew his father's body from behind as well as he knew his hands or his face. Jude's feet landed straight on the ground. Marek's step was outward-turning, like a duck's, and if he didn't concentrate, the line he'd walk would veer to the right, such was the turning of his body against nature. Jude's ankles were fine, the joint bolted and smooth, and the thin of his leg below the calf as narrow as a wrist. Marek's ankles were swollen and freckled, often scraped by briars and bleeding and itchy. His skin was thin and delicate. Ina rubbed salve on his feet from time to time to keep the skin from peeling or rotting and falling off, she said. "You're like a snake," she told him. Jude's calves were round and taut and tan, and the backs of his knees had lines from the tendons as fine as gut strings. His pants covered the rest of his legs, and were patched at the seat and between the thighs. His buttocks were high and strong. Marek knew his father's body was beautiful. But he didn't revere it. He simply respected Jude's physique as a part of nature, the way he found a vulture beautiful, or a cow. He knew that he didn't resemble his father. You couldn't compare a plover to a chicken. They were different kinds of animals. No one who saw the two together would ever guess they were of blood relation.

Jude's hips were narrow, his back was long, his shoulders strong and hunched despite their broadness, penitent. He walked with his head bowed. He took this posture having spent so many years looking down at his lambs. Sometimes Marek regarded him with admiration, a man of the harsh world who had given him a roof over his head, had mannered him in his ways, father to son. And other times Marek regarded him as a man living in the shadow of sin. He pretended to sleep while Jude molested himself every new moon under the sour woolen blanket by the fire in winter, or under the open window in spring. Summers and warm autumn nights they slept in the pasture under the stars with the lambs to make sure the wolves would stay away, Jude said. But Marek knew it was because Jude liked to feel the warm air on his skin as he slept, as though God were touching him in the breeze. Each night that Jude molested himself, he produced a baritone groan of such horror, such pain, only the Devil could be behind it, Marek thought. After the groan, Jude's body stiffened, then rocked, and it seemed to Marek that he was undergoing a spiritual ablution, as though to eject some evil from his body. Marek never let on that he knew this about his father, but he did know it. And it was yet another impediment, he believed, to the man's passage to heaven.

The sky seemed to darken now as they entered the woods. The air was chilled between the trees, no warm wind blew, but the ripeness of the earth smelled sweet and musty still. Jude preferred spring to winter. He loved the color and romance of spring. He loved the sun. Sitting and watching his lambs in an afternoon, not a shadow in sight, Jude could feel God's lips on his cheek every time he turned to face the light. That was God for him—the kiss of sun. God's hand on his bare skin was the one certainty that rose up through the abstractness of truth and thought, everything, and gave Jude a sense of belonging on Earth. He loved the grass between his toes and the soft touch of a lamb against his leg as it passed. He loved the young eyes of his babes smiling at him, their first spring, such wonder and light. He loved the ply of their joints as they moved and sniffed and chewed the sweet grass, the perk of their ears at the first songs of the titmice and chickadees on their way north. Jude's flock were polled and pure white. They were the gentlest lambs, and they stayed babes for a season longer than sheep of other origins. Even their milk teeth were rounder and flatter than others. But they were hair sheep. Not fur. They were only good for meat. So of his lambs each year, Jude kept only a few for breeding and the rest were sold for slaughter. This was the sacrifice he made, as his father had done, and his father before him. After the sale of his flock each spring, Jude tried and failed to hold his tears until he was safe and alone in his pasture with the remaining lambs—most of them would go to market next year, of course.

The lambs kept for husbandry were in mourning, too. Jude couldn't look them in the eyes. He felt guilty for having sent their brothers and sisters to be murdered. Instead of begging them for forgiveness, he treated the remaining creatures cruelly, pretending to forget them when they came in from pasture, then yelling for them to hurry up, as though they were unwanted, left over from a time he wanted to forget. But he depended on those young sheep to keep the flock of new babes on the home range. He didn't have fences out there in the pasture. He had no dog either. He understood the rhythms of grazing and thirst, and how the lambs preferred to sleep in the shade of the cottage during the day, but under the open sky at night. The babes Jude had now were only six weeks old. He'd watched the ewes' bellies grow since the fall. As the field went dormant in winter, he had fed them hay by hand, almost apologetically. "I'm sorry this isn't fresh grass and forbs." He helped to birth the babes in the lean-to, forbidding Marek to speak. "They don't like the sound of your voice," he said, and it was true. The ewes would bleat and snort and grunt if Marek came around. Jude understood that the sheep knew that Marek was a baby in his own way, that he would steal their milk for himself if he could, that he would suck the motherhood from them because he was so starving for it. "Stay away," they told him. "Baaaa."

Marek did nurse the ewes when Jude wasn't looking. He pushed the babes away and put his mouth to the sheep's teat and sucked until he felt sick. He felt this was his right as a child of God. He was a lamb himself. Not that his meekness stemmed from weakness. Rather, he was a bridled boy, gentled to be a servant to God. And as God's meek servant, this sheep's milk was his inheritance. Anything could be cajoled into sense if he thought enough about it. As father and son now walked through the woods toward the pasture, Jude was troubled by the number of shoe prints he saw dotting the path. He hoped they were not the tax collector's. He had paid all he could that spring already. Any more and he and his boy would starve.

Contrary to his father, Marek preferred winter to spring. He enjoyed the cold. He understood that God's love burned through the fire in the hearth. He liked the large kindness of that, and so he loved the smell of smoke. He liked the wet of mucus on his lip, how it would crust and pull at his skin and sting when he widened his mouth into a smile. He liked the snow on the boughs and the look of clouds, like a curtain that could be peeled back. A clear blue sky was hard to take. Marek saw it as emptiness, a place with no heaven in it. He preferred the clouds because he could imagine paradise behind them. He could stare up and focus his eyes on shapes in the clouds, wonder if that was God's face or God's hand making an impression, or if God was spying down at him through the gauzy mist. Maybe, maybe. The heavy cloak he wore in winter weighted him with comfort. If Jude loved the stinging whip, Marek loved the cold for its cruelty. He would suffer, endure it, and thereby increase his score of good deeds and humility. Without that cruel wind, there was no need for protection to be met with a fire in the hearth, there was no prayer to be answered. The oil lamp burned with precision. Its flame was female, thoughtful, like a spirit exacting its will against time. The fire in the hearth was masculine, powerful, instinctual, tireless. Marek never shivered from cold. He felt more at ease in the cold, in fact, as though his eyes could see more sharply, he could hear more clearly, everything pure and clean in the snow and crystal air.

Jude thought the spiky shadows of the trees on the snow were menacing, that the cold welcomed evil, a ghost released in every exhalation. Because things died in winter. There were no flowers, no fruit. There were no leaves on the trees. In summer, Jude was more relaxed. He went bare-chested through the field, his skin got brown and hard, his hair got light. In winter, he was stiff in his coat over layers of wool, never changed his long underwear, afraid to be naked against the chill. Marek had been born in February. Of course, he and his father never marked the occasion as the day of his birth, but the day of Agata's death. Her absence hung over both of them like a hovering bird. Marek felt the bird wasn't close enough, that it was just out of reach, that if it descended a bit farther he could grab hold of its foot and it would take him away, fly him to some better place. And Jude felt the bird was too close. If he looked up at it, it would scratch his eyes out. The difference was that Jude had known Agata. And he knew the truth about her absence. All Marek knew was that she had given her life for his own, like any good mother would do. ✦

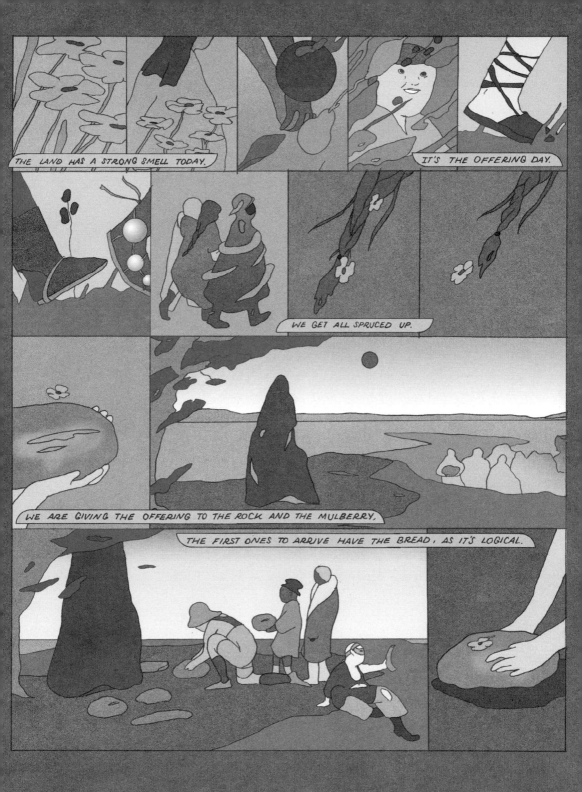

RITES OF SPRING   María Medem

THEY FINISH BAKING AT DAWN.

THE STREETS SMELL OF BREAD AND THE BIRDS HAVE STARTED TO SING SO DESPERATELY.

I CARRY THE USUAL, SILKWORMS.

THEY EAT THE MULBERRY LEAVES.

THE SKIN IS SOFT AND THIN AND IT OPENS LIKE A FLOWER, ALMOST WITHOUT EFFORT.

SUBLET
Kate Zambreno

IT WAS JUST at the start of 2020 that I met for coffee with my Swedish translator, Helena Fagertun, who was visiting New York at the time. I seldom ventured out alone socially, still hadn't figured out how to be separated from my three-year-old daughter for long periods, but I agreed to meet Helena because she had agreed to come near me. This was often my constraint for "meeting for coffee": it had to be either in my neighborhood or a neighborhood nearby. I was curious what it would be like to have a conversation with someone who had spent so much time with books I had written. I hadn't spent much time with either of these books since I wrote them, more than a decade before. Helena had rewritten them in her own language much more recently, so really, in some ways, I'm realizing while writing this, she was more recently the author of these books than I was. Perhaps I was curious to talk to someone who had spent so much time with books that I used to reside within and did no longer. If I'm being honest, I also wanted to meet with her because I wanted her to translate more of my books, especially the novel that was set to be published later that spring, which featured a scene in which the narrator, who might or might not be me, muses about the experience of having books published in Swedish, and then being written about in the Swedish media, the bubbling sense that the press is writing about someone else. In that novel I, or the I that is the narrator, am pregnant with my, or her, first child, and here I was, at the time of my meeting for coffee with Helena, in the fog of an early second pregnancy, which I was still trying to conceal, for various reasons, but which made any exoduses outside the apartment, into the freezing surprise of the open air, or the stale smells of noisy interiors, almost unbearable. Although I've become accustomed to playing the loquacious guide in most social interactions, at least with other writers, perhaps now always the professor, I found myself, at least in the one version of my memory that I recall now, without many words, almost absent of speech. When I first became a published writer, more than a decade ago, I was taken aback by how charismatic writers were supposed to be in public, when in my experience the state of being a writer is allowing long periods of being without words, whether through struggle or as a respite, it depends. I have found that I am capable of being chatty, but that I will need to repair within myself afterward, if at all possible, which is increasingly more difficult with two small children and not many places to escape to. The adjunct professor and the published writer, both of which I am, have much in common, I'm realizing as I write this. They are always expected to perform something like brilliance—as well as warmth and charm—in order to be allowed to continue, to continue being hired to teach, and continue being published, both without ongoing contracts. In a way, I wonder how much my personality has evolved by being constantly in a service role, and now I'm also a mother, a steward to others' needs and feelings. Perhaps this is also how a translator feels, that she is in service to the text, that this is a role partially of self-abnegation, however potentially pleasurable, but not without its alienation. Perhaps a Swedish translator might feel differently from an American writer, within our different economies? None of this I asked Helena Fagertun, or at least not exactly, but I thought about it during our coffee, also wondering how much she got paid to translate one of my words, versus how much I got paid to write one, but then, of course, I got paid again, usually a modest but welcome amount, to have someone else rewrite my words in another language. Perhaps this city has ruined me to art, all I think about is money and how I can get more of it.

When meeting with Helena, I knew I needed to play the part of the author of the books she had translated, and I wonder whether my presence was disappointing for her, or whether I seemed enough like myself, or the version of myself that she expected. Again, I don't remember. I've found in the past two years all memories have become somewhat disoriented. If I'm trying to remember being out in the world before the world changed, especially just before the world changed, I often try to remember where my daughter was at the time, where she was located in the margins of my consciousness. No doubt Helena Fagertun in her own recollection would have a different read on our meeting. It was, I believe, entirely pleasant, and I had no knowledge that this would be one of my last encounters with someone new for some time. I ordered a cappuccino, though I could hardly tolerate it. I remember Helena as self-contained and fairly quiet, but that could have been the language difference, if there was a language difference, or perhaps she was also jet-lagged. I remember asking her more questions than she asked of me, but that felt only fair, she after all knew a lot about me, or at least had access to the interiority in my books, and I knew nothing about her, except that she had translated two of my books and that she lived in Sweden, although I didn't even ask her where, I assumed Stockholm, which I had visited, a decade ago, back when I traveled. I vaguely remember my three-year-old running in with her father and saying, as if coached, "Hi, Helena." I remember feeling confused at Helena's apparent surprise that I had a small child, and sensed perhaps—and I'm most likely projecting—that this dislocated her sense of who I was. Since the works she had translated were written a decade earlier, drawing on material from years prior to that, perhaps Helena was surprised I was older than she had anticipated. My daughter would have known the name Helena, as this was the name of the sixteen-year-old daughter of the family next door, who during her year and a half at home regularly practiced extremely loudly in her punk band, playing mostly Hole covers, thus reliving her parents' youth, which was also my own, I hope with some knowing irony, although it was hard to tell, a constant negotiation not to wake up our daughter, whose room was closest to the noise, at first over text with Helena and later with her parents, including her father, a tech lawyer who wrote to us, without any irony, "They are just trying to exist and make art under capitalism." Things have settled between us, though, and Helena now ends before our children's bedtime, and I listen to the vibrations of the walls with some tenderness. I don't remember telling this other Helena, my Swedish translator, that I was pregnant, although I might have, it's possible I felt comfortable confessing something to her I had not shared with many others, mostly out of superstition because of my age, which increased the risk of something going wrong, or so I was warned by others, namely that horde of others, the internet. I had turned forty-two weeks earlier. If I did say something, I wasn't aware that it had any effect on her, she possibly found this confession inappropriate, as we were complete strangers, but that wasn't true either, we weren't quite strangers to each other, but I wasn't quite sure what the relationship was. There was an intimacy there, however unbalanced. I probably felt I could be candid with Helena because it felt inevitable that she would be reading about it anyway, especially as I so often did draw from my daily life, especially in the recent books. I remember she told me of the trip she was to take to Montana, a pilgrimage to the landscape of another author she was translating. An American had told her that when she was out West, she must look up, because so much of the vista was about the openness, the unbroken sky. I loved hearing about that. Later, when she wrote me an email, she attached a series of photographs dominated by a saturated blue sky, with floating wisps of clouds, the foreground a carpet of snow that looked almost like sand, in the distance rolling hills. All I could focus on, it's true, was the openness of the sky, how it filled the frame. During my first pregnancy, which I wrote about in the novel Helena hadn't yet read when we met for coffee, I often felt claustrophobic in my body and in the enclosed spaces of temporary offices where I was teaching, on train cars when I was commuting, in my own apartment where I was attempting to exist, and I would dream of vistas such as these, the openness of such space, almost like the promise of a blank page. The only time I had been in such vastness was on a trip to Scandinavia a decade earlier, the last time I had really traveled out of the country. Perhaps Helena was more used to the vastness than I was. But how would she know about my own specific fantasies of being out West, that I would dream about landscapes like that, she hadn't yet read the novel, which I hoped she would want to translate. The stretch of space was what I still dreamed about, living in this city, as well as being allowed a stretch of time, having young children and just, yes, trying to exist and make art under capitalism. In my second pregnancy I stopped dreaming of vastness, most likely because it became impossible. We spoke, Helena and I, about landscape and sky, and also Nathalie Léger's journey to the United States to repeat the pilgrimage of Barbara Loden's character Wanda in her film of the same name. At our coffee I encouraged Helena to write her own book about this author, to keep a notebook about the process of translating her, a journal of the Western landscape, but now I wonder at my arrogance or, if not arrogance, unknowingness. There is a mystery to translation, to entering a work deeply, knowing it, perhaps more than the original writer. It isn't actually my voice that the Swedish readers read, it is Helena's, or Helena somehow channeling mine, some alchemy of the two of us together, residing on the page. How does she do this? What magic happens in this process? The rewriting that is translating is a writing that is closer to reading, which is closer to the writing I wish to do. The translating self is an invisible visitor within the text. It was arrogant to assume that Helena wished for the self in this transformation to be made more visible. This was the individualistic, capitalist approach to literature I have been of late trying to rid myself of, and why I was actively seeking out forms of collaboration and community. It was a brief meeting with Helena, no longer than an hour. I haven't returned to the bookstore where we had coffee since then, though it used to be a place I frequented. Nor, I believe, have I had a coffee out with another writer, but my memory of this is also like a morning fog, and then it dissipates, and I'm unsure whether time has passed at all, or how much time has passed since I've been social, outside of my intimate family life and the occasional playdate. Afterward we each wrote each other the now customary follow-up, How nice to see you! She enclosed her photographs, and I enclosed, rather pushily, the proof of my novel, which was published later that spring, in the hope that she would read it, while knowing also the burden of expectation this entailed. I should mention that in our meeting I never got the sense from Helena of her feelings toward me, or should I say my work, although I'm assuming she felt fond of the original, at least in some way. There is a romantic idea that one translates out of love, but I know it's also out of labor and obligation. I imagine her feeling toward my writing was one of ambivalence, sometimes frustration and irritation, that she was aware of my tics, of the overuse of certain words or phrases, why for example, do my sentences have to go on and on. I wonder if there's anyone who has read my work more closely or more intimately, in order to imagine how she would rewrite it. If she read the novel that I sent her, would she read it in the voice in which she'd translate it, which was in a way her own? Of the earlier works, I cringe at the culs-de-sac, the attempts at profundity, the wobbly sentences she would no doubt improve upon. Helena did end up writing me, some time later, that she had read my new novel, and was taken by the opening, where I had written about Rilke looking at the purple heather on his desk, which reminded him of the rural landscapes he'd inhabited with his estranged wife, Clara. It's so strange, wrote Helena, I have just published an essay in a journal here thinking through the motif—I believe she wrote motif—of heather in Swedish literature by women writers. I couldn't believe this when I read it—that we were both thinking of heather at the same time. The purple incense-scented sprig of heather decorated both of our desks, so to speak, over space and time. Helena attached her essay in the email, apologizing, knowing I couldn't read it, as it was in Swedish. I could see how beautifully laid out it was, with little heather icons dividing the sections. My own book was published, and I began to do events, at home, because we were all inside, arranged heavily pregnant on my couch in just the right light, my face gleaming with exertion, speaking to people through the screen, and I would see Helena's name pop up as an audience member, and wonder ambiently what time it was for her, as it must have been the middle of the night.

More than a year later we corresponded again, as Helena was in fact going to translate the new novel for a new Swedish publisher, which I was pleased by. In the midst of a warm and courteous exchange, Helena mentioned that she hoped to be in the city again this summer, and asked if I knew of anyone looking to sublet their apartment in August. I wrote to her that actually, we might be trying to visit family in the Midwest, after not leaving the city for more than a year, and then offered that she could stay here, at my home, if she wanted, without us there. Of course, I wrote to Helena, you might not want to stay in an apartment where the largest room, which used to be my office, is now devoted to my two young daughters. We could, I found myself thinking later, find a way to put in our already overstuffed closets the baskets of children's toys, and clothes et cetera, to find a way to return it to a home where only adults lived, to return it I suppose in some ways to the home it was before I had children, to the home described in my novel that she would be translating. Helena wrote that she would love to sublet the apartment, if it all worked out. The more I thought about it, the more excited I was by the idea. I previously would never have allowed someone to sublet my home, as the idea of strangers occupying my space, inhabiting my bed, disturbed me. The unpleasant feeling that someone had slept in my bed and had existed in my space felt wonderfully strange when thinking about Helena Fagertun there. It made me regard my home in a new way, as if charged with a different energy. Although many people I knew seemed to be moving on—entering other interior spaces—I had not. I still lived a sealed, almost hermetic existence, one of mostly being inside the apartment, working, still speaking to screens, or if I ventured outside, it was with the children, walking in the neighborhood or spending time in the park. Life went on—the destabilizing hammer of the drill outside, breaking up the sidewalk—but I was still here. We had not left. In fact, we had not had anyone else inside for two years. But how unusual was that really, we weren't social in that way. Helena could come and inhabit my space, and it would have to, at least temporarily, become her space as well. She would be doing her own thinking and reading and writing here, but it would be in a space that was still filled with my presence, the vibration of the familiar objects and clutter that I have never been able to fully express in writing. The doubling she might feel, sitting on the porch with the broken chair, the same chair described in the novel, the chair where she might sit to watch the parade of dogs walking by, the soothing repetitions of a neighborhood that provided the setting and energy for the novel that she would be translating. And wasn't this what translating was, occupying someone else's space, rewriting and moving around sentences, or like relocating one's furniture and objects from one dwelling to another dwelling in another city while attempting to reconstruct the same feeling of home. However, imagining this, I felt suddenly self-conscious about how she would regard my space, the judgments she might make. I imagined she might be drawn to the wall of filled IKEA bookshelves, that was my background on the screen, the row of bookshelves, that's all one could see. A writer surrounded by her notebooks and books, that's the dominant image people like to see. I look up from the couch to the bookshelf behind me, and scan for any Scandinavian writers in translation. I feel mildly ashamed of the scarcity. But the ones I have read are important to me. There are English translations of Tove Jansson's *The Summer Book*, the Danish writer Dorthe Nors, the Norwegian writer Gunnhild Øyehaug, the Swedish writer Sara Stridsberg. Will Helena take these paperbacks down, scan the English, does the tone come through as it should, odd and detached, or calm and contemplative? I imagine Helena reading this essay, the one I am now writing, even deciding to translate it. I imagine she will pick up each clunky sentence, each word, like the unmatched shoes thrown into my closet. As I change words, I imagine her doing this as well. Is "*loquacious* guide" really necessary? Couldn't she just write "guide"? What would Helena think of my rather haphazard interior decorating and cleaning? I try to let light in, to find pretty and light-filled corners of the apartment, I will sometimes exude energy rearranging, but in truth I spend very little time on it, and the children have taken over. There are toys all over the floor, and a pile of unfolded laundry on the table. The rugs are filthy. What kind of state will the apartment be left in? Surely we would leave in a hurry, in the night, or too late just before noon when we meant to leave in the morning. Would there be a transfer over, somehow, or would she just be given the door code, and enter the space unpeopled? Would she go into my closets, look at my clothes, the mountain of shoes, none of which fit anymore, my feet growing slightly larger with each pregnancy? I surely would, if I were subletting, especially if it were the place of the author whom I was translating. The drilling makes it impossible to think. Would she sit at my desk, which is now in the front room, underneath a window that looks upon a trash-filled alley? What kind of thinking would she do here? I only imagine her thinking alongside me, reading my work, attempting to write alongside me, but certainly she would have her own work to do as well, her other work. She'd be entering my atmosphere. Perhaps the amount of details from a noisy domestic life would be overwhelming. Would she choose to elaborate on any of them, for her translation of my work set within this space? But this life would not be that life. She would be writing about the time before I had children, when this space possessed solitude. Would she find that solitude again here? The place will change once she's inside it. And once it does, it will never be the same. I imagine her, sitting here, in a late New York summer, hearing the vibration of the other Helena playing the drums through the walls and the construction noise. It will be her, here, in this space. I will be the invisible one. ✦

DEN

Helena Fagertun

Translated from
the SWEDISH by SASKIA VOGEL

I'M SITTING ON the sofa with a sleeping cat in my lap as I recall my first encounter with Kate Zambreno. It was sometime around 2011, when I was working on a co-translation of a novel and stumbled across Zambreno's essay on the author. A few years later I found myself translating her book *Heroines*, which I had eagerly anticipated. The work was by turns obsessive and elusive, and I kept drifting away from the task at hand; I started collecting and reading each book mentioned, and I became convinced that the translation was going to drive me crazy. I imagined being better at the job if I were someone else, someone in possession of Zambreno's linguistic precision and ease in switching between more theoretical reflections, gossip from the literary world, and the quotidian. When Kate told me that she was working on a piece about translation called "Sublet," on what it would be like if, as we say in Swedish, I rented her apartment secondhand, it was as if I finally had a metaphor for translation that, appropriately enough, made me feel at home. It's less about what is lost in translation, and more about what is still there. I began drafting a translation of her as yet nonexistent piece in my head. The word *sublet* is simultaneously a noun and a verb, encompassing both the place and how that place is occupied. The English allows for a terseness lacking in its unwieldy Swedish counterpart *andrahandsuthyrning*.

When I first met Kate, on a January day in 2020, I had already read her novel *Drifts*, and it was difficult for me to separate the writer from her work. I felt that I had already spent so much time with her. She was wearing a white jumpsuit, and all I could think about was a sentence in which she confesses how carefully she dresses for other women. She apologized for being late, and remembering the animal passages in *Drifts*, I imagined her stopping to help a dog or cat on the way. Previously, I'd always found it easy to talk about Zambreno's way of blending the narrative and authorial self— the slippage between the two being what, for me, distinguished her writing. But with Kate right in front of me, I felt that I knew so very much about her and yet could not determine what to actually discuss with her. I listened and tried to answer in my best English, afraid that she would otherwise think it unreasonable that someone who spoke so haltingly could be a translator. But this also limited the possible discussions between us, limited even the thoughts that could be thought. This might have been why I didn't ask her about language—how she feels about writing in a language as dominant as English while increasingly engaging with writers who wrote in other languages, such as Rilke and Guibert. Instead, we talked about the day-to-day realities of our lives, the economic conditions of working with literature in our respective communities.

I look forward to the summer of 2022, when I'll meet with Kate again at the same café. I will have devoted the previous months to translating *Drifts* and will have parts of the text that I want to look at with her. After our coffee, she and her family will leave for the Midwest, and I'll move into their apartment. In the evening, I will take a seat on the broken chair on the porch, and a tiny cat will sneak across the grass toward me. I will realize how crucial it is that I finish writing the book, in Swedish, right here. ✦

HYPNOSIS WOMAN

Kim Hyesoon

Translated from the KOREAN by DON MEE CHOI

How do you feel? *Lonely. I feel as if I'm floating about in lukewarm water. Feels like I've become massless, weightless. Feels good.* Please return to the past. What do you see? *Light. I can keep going inside it. The light surrounds me. It's so bright that I can't look at it anymore. Please put the sleep shades on my eyes. And feminine napkins below.*

You can see but you can't speak. I ask, and you answer. You can only live in the world of answers. You eat, but I tell you what you're tasting. These shoes are delicious! When you eat the shoes, you become vivacious. You want to eat them every second—my shoes. Even my toes.

Spit. Grab tight. Walk quickly down the hallway. Your heart beats hard when I get near you. Your heart aches when I'm far away. You smile when you see me. You don't smile at just anyone.

From now on, your body will lean to the left. You can't stretch your body to the right. Your bag is dragged along on your left side. The food on the tray spills to the left. You've got a ringing in your left ear. Your beautiful right side is mine.

When I say TV, the TV hypnotizes you. When I say sewing machine, the sewing machine hypnotizes you. When I say calendar, the days from 1 to 31 hypnotize you. When I say 1, you raise both hands. When I say 5, you take off your clothes. When I say 6, you open your legs. Now, the numbers are commands. You're not permitted to open your bag. My voice is inside your bag. Wipe your tears with your hand. You're surrounded by my replacements.

You can't interrupt my speech. You're a one-person space shuttle circling above the infinite orbit. You can only respond to me or NASA. You can't return without me now. At last, your heart's hypnotizing you, isn't it? Your heart only responds to me regardless of your own will. Try shouting after me. My heart is yours. *My heart is yours.*

Repeat!
I'm your goosebumps!
I'm your orgasm!
I'm your pocket!

You're tired now. Your legs are relaxed. Your eyelids keep drooping. Moonlight puts you to sleep. Are you asleep? Good. You'll forget about today. You'll wake up after the third knock. When you awake, you won't remember me. As you take off your shades, you might have an inkling of something.

—The night wind is quiet. The wind that doesn't carry a command is not a wind. Water tastes really great! Where did the person who told me this go? Without the commands I'm not me. Water tastes like water. Since no one tells me, Now you can take one small step and walk out, I'm not me. I'm nothing like the mirror on the wall. The voice that said, Climb, climb up the hypnosis, the voice that lived inside me, has vanished. I'm not real without the voice that took me to that place instantly. Without the no command I'm not even no.

THIS IS HEAVEN

Nada Alic

ILLUSTRATION BY Franz Lang

"DON'T STOP UNTIL you recognize me."

We do this every Sunday afternoon, as if our lives depended on it. Jordan strains his face like he has to pee but he's holding it in. I watch him squirm and settle into a seated position on the floor. We're performing a meditation technique I half read about in a magazine and half invented myself based on years of self-taught online Buddhist study. How it works is you take an object and focus on it until it's no longer that object, but something else. It's a form of unlearning that loosens up your mental associations and frees you from the attachments that no longer serve you. Depending on how advanced you are, you can turn something as ordinary as a toothbrush into a special healing wand or the sudden feeling of immense gratitude. I can do it with almost anything now. I can turn a stick of gum into a satisfying meal. I can look at Jordan's face and see my soulmate.

"Okay," he says.

We conduct the exercise by sitting across from each other on the living room floor. I like to break him up into parts and slowly work my way up to his whole being. It's like looking at a Magic Eye—revealing a depth that appears only when you're paying attention. I bet he takes me in all at once, the way he does with everything: how he inhales food like a hungry stoner, or in bed, the way he yanks my underwear to the side and jams himself in. There's no right way to do it other than sitting and staring until it's over. Meaning, we've found each other again. Sometimes he sees me immediately and has to sit and wait until I'm ready. The longest we ever went was around two hours but that's because I got bangs and he was having a hard time finding me under them.

I begin with his lips. They are thin, bright pink, and chapped, and I can tell they're hiding something. I squint until all of his other features blur and disappear and then I attempt to communicate with his mouth telepathically. After twenty seconds, the disembodied mouth starts laughing uncontrollably, excited by its newfound emancipation from the face. I remain calm and try to ask it things like, "Do you love me or are you just afraid to die alone?" and, "Why won't you let me touch your asshole?" But it's too distracted to answer. It quickly grows confident, repeating "cunt" and "motherfucker" over and over again, like a tic. I realize the mouth on its own has nothing to tell me, and place it back onto the face with a firm blink.

A strobe of afternoon light cuts through the window, illuminating thousands of dust particles descending upon our jute rug. I swallow a cough and wonder how much dust I've eaten in my lifetime. Several pounds, at least. The microscopic film coats every surface of our modest apartment, the one we've shared for the past six years and never thought to leave because rent in the neighborhood has doubled in the past two years alone. Just like that, our apartment has become highly coveted real estate. I think about this whenever I hear the elderly widow above us farting loudly in her kitchen or screaming Slavic insults into her telephone. *Pizda materina!* "This is heaven. I'm in heaven," I repeat to myself as I crush another silverfish with a giant wad of paper towel only to watch it crawl triumphantly out of the trash can, disfigured and limping. We're royalty, in a sense, and even though we've done nothing to earn it, we agree that on a cosmic level, we have. Friends anxiously wait for us to leave: find a duplex in the suburbs and move on with our lives. What they don't know is that we've agreed to grow old and die in this apartment together, no matter what.

Most couples never see it coming: that thing that blooms over years like mold, making them lazy and forgetful. It got so bad for our downstairs neighbor Geoffrey that he confused a woman he met online for his wife, Eleanor. He eventually moved in with this woman, claiming he was no longer convinced that Eleanor was who she said she was. Well, she was. I saw her yesterday. How do you just forget a person like that?

Some days I can see him so clearly, my husband, but then he shape-shifts into a child with a fever, or a slob roommate, or a chatty girlfriend. Or worse: an appendage of mine, some human-shaped growth with hair and teeth that spooks me every time it brushes against my leg in bed. We even have our own language: a garbled baby talk that doesn't so much communicate meaning but evokes a general mood. *Pleebo, Boobkus, Moosh,* and so forth. We are like two wounded children. My therapist calls it "enmeshment." It's embarrassing, but I can't stop.

Jordan never cared much for meditating but is willing to try anything to save our marriage. Maybe *save* isn't the right word for it, rather: *sustain, nourish, grow.* "Safe words," he jokes. He's an obedient partner and agrees with me on nearly every topic except when it comes to my body, which he worships despite its obvious and well-documented defects. Specifically, my most problematic areas: the cellulite under my ass, how when I lie on my back, my nothing little breasts disappear into my chest, the disappointing ways my skin betrays me despite a rich diet of retinoids and sunscreen. His defense always feels personal, as if I were offending someone who was not me—an orphan or some omnipotent god figure. I can't trust that kind of confidence.

As a rule, we approach matters of the heart with caution. We both suffered the indignities of online dating after thirty and emerged too wounded to talk about what we'd seen, fixating instead on easier topics like the state of our gut flora or thoughtful ways to reduce our carbon footprint. Crawling, just barely, off the battlefields of our twenties, we were embarrassingly ill-equipped for the bigness of love. The brutal heft of it. I couldn't bear it, not for a lifetime. I need a careful love, a reliable witness. No one says this out loud, they just know it. You get tired of chasing the ghost and then you trust fall into the arms of whoever will catch you. It's a survival skill, a way to eliminate risk. I told Jordan my entire sexual history on our first date, hoping that he'd find my display of forced intimacy endearing, and not manipulative, as a former therapist once labeled it. Still, it took him years to reveal that his previous and only girlfriend left him for a female lifeguard, forcing him to reconfigure his jealousy to include both men and women. He avoids public pools now, says the smell of chlorine gives him a headache. It's an unwanted feeling, like a fear of dogs after an unprovoked attack by the family pet.

Ours is an uncomplicated love, aside from the occasional flare-up we offer each other: an email from Jordan's ex-girlfriend asking for her copy of *The Artist's Way* back, or a recurring sex dream about a cousin that haunts me for weeks. Despite our precautions, we started losing each other under layers of performance fleece and reruns of British procedurals. Our sex, too, is predictable and choreographed. I could do it with my eyes closed and often will. I like imagining other people on top of me, like his father, so that I could be the one to give birth to Jordan and raise him to be more self-assured and independent. Less sensitive to criticism, also dairy.

When my mind wanders like this, I wiggle my toes to return to my body. I ground myself in space and time by relaxing my eyes to get a full view of the room without breaking my focus. The first thing I notice is an industrial steampunk-looking lamp that needs a special bulb I never got around to buying. I thought it was cool just a few months ago and now every time I look at it, I want to hurl it out the window. How could I have been so wrong? I usually have discerning taste but occasionally I surprise myself with an impulsive chevron print or something macramé and worry that I actually have no idea who I am or what I like. I strain my eyeballs to the edge of my peripheral vision, where a clock sits on a mantel, but it's just a white orb with no numbers. How long has it been? I'm already bored, so bored, so bored.

The sound of Jordan shifting his weight brings me back and I unrelax my gaze and bring my focus back to him. Hello, hi. I'm here. I look down at his chest and notice he's wearing my beige sweater. I like the way it drapes over his pointed shoulders. I like a thin man, almost sickly-looking. It makes him look so graceful, like a dancer. We share clothes, mostly neutral-colored cotton basics from Uniqlo; that way we don't have to expend energy picking out what to wear in the morning. It's more efficient since we both work from home. Jordan scores film and transitional music for reality TV and I work part-time for an environmental advocacy group. So while the planet cooks and world leaders threaten global annihilation, we've resigned ourselves to an indoor life, thoughtfully constructing our own private paradise in uncertain times.

Sometimes I worry we've done too good a job and we'll never want to leave again. Our efforts to safeguard against loneliness made us too dependent on each other, causing a self-perpetuating loop. The more together we are, the more we shut out the world, the more we distrust it, the more we need each other, et cetera. I'm finding it harder and harder to go outside when everything I need is right here. Every room has been optimized for maximum efficiency and comfort: a black-and-white dish set, a single bread knife, a fake fig tree by the window, a tweed love seat and a glass coffee table and a closet filled with expensive Canadian wool blankets. We're both inspired by Kanso and *wabi-sabi* design, but Jordan made me get rid of our bonsai tree out of a sensitivity toward cultural appropriation. At the start of every season, we like to reset by purging all of our nonessential belongings and surrounding ourselves with objects that evoke joy. The goal is to eventually want for nothing. The goal is to be free.

This controlled environment works for now, but what about the future? Who will we be? My future self is capable of anything and I hate her for that. I've heard stories about men who emerge from botched brain surgery as pedophiles, and no one knows why. Or those women who smother their husbands with pillows or sleepwalk into the ocean. When I shared my concerns with an online chat room for advanced meditators, a few of them suggested I incorporate the drug ecstasy into my practice to encourage deep feelings of empathy and connection with my partner. Jordan had never done it and the one time I did, I slow danced with a coatrack alone in a hotel room, sobbing. I remember it being cathartic. I eventually managed to procure some pills from my niece's boyfriend Chad, but whatever he gave me must have been cut with amphetamines, because instead of meditating we took turns picking at the shower grit, scrubbing the walls, and wiping dust off the venetian blinds until there was nothing left to wipe. I stayed up all night listening to the sound of Jordan slapping his dry tongue against the roof of his mouth while I heard a symphony coming from inside my own brain. I'm worried I caused us permanent brain damage.

I look down at Jordan's folded legs and try not to laugh; nothing is funny, but my restless body is filled with so much energy that it sometimes expresses itself without my consent. The sitting is so uncomfortable it's impossible not to laugh or cry or hum a little tune. My body will do anything to cut through the silence. Jordan almost laughs but it dies in his throat, choked out by his enormous Adam's apple. I immediately think of the saddest thing I can think of: Jordan as a toddler waving goodbye to his mother as she pulls out of the driveway and never comes back. His baby cheeks pressed up against the foggy glass. "Ma-ma!" he screams in an empty living room. This never happened, but it helps me to recalibrate. I return his gaze with renewed seriousness. I fix my eyes on his nose and wait for a revelation, some recognition of our truest selves, and by that I mean the best versions of ourselves: the ones that were advertised to us, promised to us in front of God and everyone we know. I think if we look hard enough and really focus, we can remember who those people are and how to coax them out. Maybe we'll discover we're sex positive or into vape culture; I'm open to all possibilities.

I stare into his eyes, which are wide and expressionless, like a curious toddler's or a benevolent monk's. His eyes are always watching me in a sort of all-loving, all-knowing kind of way. "You've got an eyelash," he'll say, "make a wish!" then present it to me on his finger, things like that. He has monitored my every move over the years—from the way I incorrectly lift an Amazon package (legs, not back!) to the irregularity of my menstrual cycle to the way I walk slow "on purpose"—as if he were taking notes for a research study on the most inept woman alive.

In retaliation, I take secret pleasure in making him cry. I'm not proud of this, but I've accumulated a greatest hits of insults that can make it happen on command. I'll say things like, "You've told us this one already," after he shares another depressing story about his dad's beloved Jamaican hospice nurse to all of our friends over happy hour drinks. When he later tells me I hurt his feelings, I'll roll my eyes and tell him to grow up, which makes no sense since he's seven years older than me and has high cholesterol. I'll mention that, too. I know it's coming when he looks up at the ceiling to keep his tears from falling, hoping they might reabsorb back into his head. The look of anguish and betrayal on his face transforms him and he once again becomes a stranger to me. Immediately I fall at his feet and beg for forgiveness. My sweet Boobkus! Remember me? Making him cry for sport is both immensely pleasurable and physically unbearable. It's the closest I've ever felt to being in love.

"Now?" he whispers.

I shake my head, no.

His face barely even looks human now, more like a mound of clay. I rub my eyes and look again. When I do, another man's face appears, someone I've never met before. He looks as menacing as a serial killer or a lonely youth pastor. I start to worry that I'm hallucinating, that I've gone too far and lost my grip on reality. I believe this happens to advanced sitters, but because I'm a novice, it startles me. I look down at the ground and work my way back up again, hoping to snap out of it, but this time I see my college boyfriend Rico flexing his bicep and looking constipated. "Sup," he proclaims. It's just like Rico to show up like that, in a manner that feels forced and nonconsensual. I blink again and there's Jordan looking back at me, totally oblivious.

Let me think: Jordan. Love of my life. I search inside the creases of his eyes, his defined jowl. I stare at the pink mole protruding from the side of his left nostril. Every time I look at it, I have a deep animal desire to rip it off. He looks panicked but hopeful, as if he fears being lost forever. I panic, too, but don't show it. I'm determined to see him, really see him. Who am I looking for, anyway? I want the old Jordan, still perfect and unencumbered by my petty judgments. This was the same Jordan who had yet to discover my night terrors or my eczema or my student loan debt. The Jordan who inspired me to take up reading for maybe the first time in my life, just to impress him. *Tolstoy? Yes, looove it. Him. Love him.* The Jordan whose car seats and armpits and bath towels smelled like some heavenly combination of cologne and sweat; it gave me a drug-like high. It made me want to breathe until I passed out.

Suddenly, I hear what sounds like a synthy electronic beat playing through the vents and just like that, I remember the night we went dancing in a dark club, or rather I was dancing and he was sort of hovering over me, holding my hips, swaying awkwardly from side to side. We never go dancing, we aren't those people, but we decided to try it one night after dinner, the way tourists might wander curiously into ornate cathedrals hoping to spontaneously feel the presence of God. "What if it's fun?" he proposed, looking drunk and cross-eyed. Once we entered the club, we quickly realized that we were surrounded by sexy youths and professional dancers and our version of dancing wasn't funny at all, it was humiliating. "I thought I was good!" I shouted. "But I'm actually bad!" He took my hand and twirled me to the tune of an imaginary polka beat as trap music thudded our rib cages.

"You're the best one here!" he said. I fell into his arms and wept.

When I come to, he gives me a confused look, which I assume means that he's lost me. I'm taking forever, and it reminds him of how slow I am at most things. I forgot that I'm also being watched and the realization horrifies me. Is my mascara doing that thing where it smears around my eyes and makes me look goth? Do I look too much like his mother now? Does he wish I looked more like her? What's my hair doing? Did I even try to fix it? I feel exposed, as if all my flaws are on display at once, even the internal ones. I wonder if it shows on my face: My secret browser history. The contents of my manifestation journal. That ancestral rage in my blood that emerges randomly, like when we're playing cards. Or how I've changed, seemingly overnight, and I don't know how to stop. Can he see, too, that I'm trying? That I want to be good? I relax my face and perform a childlike smile.

The longer I sit, the less I recognize him. Even little things lose their context, a side effect of staring at anyone for too long. What are bodies? And what is a hand, anyway? Is it a hand, or is it a family of fingers? I imagine him dying in front of me. The hiss of his last breath, his lifeless body. It's an old body, with spots and craters and pustules all over it. I'm afraid to touch it or go near it. I'm afraid of its coldness, its strange smell. I sit and wait and watch until he slowly comes back to life, filling up with blood, growing younger. I watch the spots disappear and he is himself again, breathing effortlessly. I'm relieved, but I can't unsee it: how it ends, right here in the living room.

The distance between us grows and grows until it becomes an ever-expanding, gaping canyon with exquisite vistas. Jordan is a dot, barely visible to the human eye. I sit on the edge of a cliff and wave violently in the hopes that he might see me. If I can't find my way back, then what? What happens to two people separated by some abstract, unmeasurable distance? My Buddhist video tutorials taught me that meditation, or really any kind of intense, singular focus could cure anything: anxiety, food allergies, you name it. I briefly consider the possibility of being wrong.

The sun is setting. We hadn't thought to turn on the light and it is getting dark, but neither of us can move. Moving doesn't even seem like an option. The man in my living room scratches the tip of his nose. The problem is his nose isn't where it's supposed to be, it's been grotesquely flipped and jumbled like a Cubist painting. His one eye hangs low on his left cheek and his ear floats above his head. It's as if my brain had taken his individual features and scattered them at random. I sit waiting for the night to erase him in a sheet of darkness.

"You still there?" I ask.

"Yeah, are you?"

"Yep."

"Can I turn the light on?" he asks.

"Please!"

Jordan gets up and flicks on the light switch while I rub my legs and come back into my body. Then he looks at me. "Well?" he says. "Did you see me?"

I never did. I saw him only once, on our first sitting. There it was: his soul. It happened so fast, like a shooting star or a head-on collision. Gone in a blink.

"Yeah," I say, "I saw you."

He smiles, then looks down and notices a giant brown beetle sauntering across our laminate tiles. It senses its being watched and freezes. Without saying a word, Jordan slowly picks up his slipper and crushes it with an impressive blow. When I get up to look, the beetle's amputated antennae are still twitching and its iridescent shell has torn into bits of cellophane, covered in goo. I stand back and watch as he wipes up the guts with a paper towel and washes his hands meticulously, like a surgeon. I know I might never see him again, but I want to spend my whole life trying. ⨎

PAIN LIKE A PHILOSOPHY

Chinelo Okparanta

ILLUSTRATION BY Diana Ejaita

IF YOU PASS the asphalt lot overgrown with weeds, walk beyond the acorn-strewn nursery, and cross the field littered with picnic benches and barbecue grills, you will find yourself on Sligo Creek Trail. I have walked these woods for twelve months, watching the moths and the black hawks, the red cardinals and gray swallows, the glistening rocks that line the creek. I have regarded my reflection in the silver water—a thin silhouette, yellow-pale under the sun's glow, different from what it used to be. In the Igbo language there are expressions that contemplate distance. *Agbacha oso a guo mile.* It is only after the race that the distance covered is calculated. And yet, I track my steps as I walk. I check my pedometer for the accumulation of each tenth of a mile.

In the Igbo language, there are expressions, also, that contemplate suffering. I have suffered these twelve months. I have wasted away, endured the kind of pain that does not allow one the enjoyment of life. Good health eludes me still. But there is nothing unique about my suffering. We have all suffered. *Ejighi ahuhu etu onu.* One must not boast of suffering.

The burning in my chest and abdomen has been as invasive as the pandemic itself. In the more recent months, the most profound pain has become the fear of a pain that refuses to end. I have questioned my purpose, questioned God, questioned life, questioned love, questioned death, questioned pain.

Pain like a scorching of skin and chest. I whirl inside of it, splashing, crawling, submerged in it, pain like a hot cauldron of water and I a crab. I am out of breath with it. Pain like a philosophy, a gift of sensation, a cruel reminder that I am alive.

The mind sickens itself in the body's misery. If my mind senses a physical pain, is the pain really there? Does the intensity of the pain measure the intensity of the physical damage? If I believe that the body heals itself, is the mere belief enough to heal me? If I believe I am made in the image of God, am I, then, also a god? Will I, then, get to live eternally, as most gods do? Above all, where is God's love in all of this? But then again, *o bu mmuo ndi na-efe na-egbu ha.* It is the deity that people worship that kills them.

What I am certain of each time I walk is that I don't want to die before I die. And so I trudge along. *Onye nwuru anwu si, "Ihe ibu, abugom. Ihe mbu ka ika abu."* The dead man says, "What you are, I have already been, but what I am, you are yet to be."

Today, long before I reach my first mile, the pain becomes more intense than ever. Pain like coarse sand scattered inside my chest. Pain like shards of glass making tiny slits within the delicate walls of my esophagus. I crouch in the corner of the trail where the children's pink-and-yellow chalk markings do not reach. Just then, my phone rings. Consy has never called before during my walk. She makes it a point not to interrupt what we agree is a sort of meditation. But today, she has somehow intuited my pain, and she has called to check on me. All my life, she has been checking on me.

I see her in my mind's eye: my mother crouched in a praying position, praying over me. Consy seated on the edge of the sofa, face covered in tears, because she has been waiting for me. It is hours after my doctor's appointment, and she has called and called, and I have not answered. She doesn't know that my phone, not her daughter, is dead. Consy and I on our trips back home to Port Harcourt, to Lagos, to Ojoto, seated side by side on the airplane, in the car. "Ruth and Naomi", my siblings still tease us. Consy seated on the faux fur chair in my living room, chatting riotously about her love for Patience Ozokwor, trying her best to distract me from my fears. Consy talking to her peace lily and Blue Angel plants as she waters them. "What wonders only a little sunlight and water will do!" Consy telling me about her infamous pound cake and meat pie recipes, telling me that she will make them for me as soon as I am better. "So hurry up and get better." Consy singing to me in her high-pitched squealing voice. "Healing, Healing, Healing, Spirit, mind and body, mind and body, you are healed, through the wonder working power . . . Great Jehovah you are healed . . ." "Sing up!" she says to me. "There's nothing more time-tested than the power of song to heal!" Then she holds a towel over my head above a bucket of hot water. "Breathe deeply," she says. With so much hope that the remedy would be as easy as that.

I am forty years old. I have played the role of second mother, godmother, auntie, big sister, teacher, mentor, solid friend to many, but in that moment, by the side of the trail, I am a helpless child. And I feel Consy's love profoundly. I feel it even in that small word: "Binto," she says, her nickname for me. "Should I come pick you up?"

"No," I tell her, because with her voice on the phone, the pain recedes. Agaracha must come back. She who wanders must eventually return. As if I were wandering toward her, I wander back to my home.

On my way, I see her reflection in my reflection in the creek. I am my mother's daughter, and I must not let her down; I must live. I once read somewhere that in order to discover God you must descend into yourself, to your lowest self. You must experience the lowest points of your humanity. Low as I am, there is a lightness in my body that leaves me strong, stronger. I sense my self elevated, as with God on the highest of the mountaintops. A powerful heat descends upon my head, travels down my chest, my stomach, my legs, and exits through my feet. I feel its flow like the flow of scalding water. Heat becomes numbness becomes ecstasy becomes a complete and utter awareness of the sudden absence of pain. I have always been awake, but I am now more awake than ever. I hear Consy's voice in the songs of the birds. I have smelled the late winter leaves before, and the blossoming of spring in the trees, but I have never smelled them so strongly as I do now.

The great gift of human life is consciousness. Awareness. *Agbacha oso a guo mile.* It is only after the race that the distance covered is calculated. Today, I have walked less than a mile on Sligo Creek Trail. But I have traveled far: into a more profound hope, after a terrible pain. ✦

AGAINST NOSTALGIA

Ada Limón

If I had known you were coming, back then,
when I first thought love could be the thing
to save me after all—if I had known, would I
have still glued myself to the back of his motorcycle
while we flew across the starless bridge
over the East River to where I grew
my first garden behind the wire fencing,
in the concrete raised beds lined by ruby
twilight roses? If I had known it would be you,
who even then I liked to look at, across a room,
always listening rigorously, a self-questioning look,
the way your mouth was always your mouth,
would I have climbed back on that bike again
and again until even I was sick with fumes
and the sticky seat too hot in the early fall?
If I had known, would I have still made mistake
after mistake until I had only the trunk of me left,
stripped and nearly bare of leaves myself?
If I had known, the truth is, I would have kneeled
and said, Sooner, come to me sooner.

BLOWING ON THE WHEEL

Ada Limón

It's getting late, the light's grayish gold
on the hillside and I'm thinking of car rides
from Brooklyn to the Cape, or up
to Moon Mountain from the City
or out to Stockbridge that one winter
with H and her sister and cousin
and how we called them the Stockbridges.
And I accidentally said, Have a Norman Mailer
Christmas and not a Norman Rockwell Christmas and we
laughed at how sad a Norman Mailer Christmas
would be. Or how, another time, we waited for T to put
our bags in the car as if she was not just driving, but
the driver. Or how after T got a ticket
on 6 East she'd go the speed limit but blow
on the steering wheel like it was a sail and say,

Is the car even on? The three of us,
always piling into the back of some cab
and deciding what was next, which was
never bed because there was still so
much to figure out. And how someone
once asked H if we ever just ran out of subjects
to keep talking about, and of course we wouldn't
we won't, it's endless, even this is endless,
the sky darkening in the way that makes me
wish we were wandering right now around
New York City somewhere or at the Governor Bradford
and not wandering at all, or just talking
or not talking or being happy or not unhappy,
and this is my secret work, to be worthy
of you both and this infinite discourse
where everything is interesting because you
point it out and say, *Isn't that interesting?*
And how mostly we say, Remember
that time and we will nod because we do
remember that time. Except for the few times
we've forgotten, like that one time when H
was trying to remind us of something
and when we asked her what, she said, *I don't know,*
but you were there and I was there. And we were.

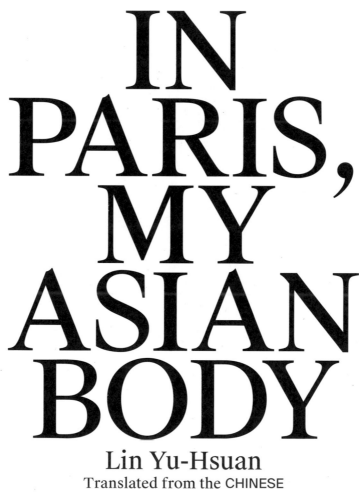

IN PARIS, MY ASIAN BODY

Lin Yu-Hsuan
Translated from the CHINESE
by CHLOE GARCIA ROBERTS

MY BODY WAS was resplendent on the bed from every angle, touched all over by the thousand needles of his delight. At the peak of my climax, I burst into an Oriental rainbow. The Moroccan man may have been watching us. The curtains absorbed the force of his stare, but passion seeped through them like water.

In the early morning I wondered, *What does my Asian body mean in Paris?*

My classmate Pierre is a beautiful man. To say he is a beautiful man is the fruit of Asian eyes contemplating a European body. His tawny lion's mane of curls, chest hair prickling out over his collar, eyes the color of an empty sky, over six feet tall—he is the model of stereotypical perfection, as if cast from a mold. The cauldron that made him opened like a clamshell and he rose from out of its depths.

My classmate Shahin is a beautiful man. To say he is a beautiful man is the fruit of Asian eyes contemplating an African body. He has hair like steel wire, radiant black skin, severe features, and meticulously groomed facial hair. He crosses the school library's glass suspension bridge, and everything around him falls away, leaving behind only the lustrous pearls of his eyes.

Pierre loves to say, *Je suis désargenté*—my silver leaf has come off. The way his whole person gleamed, it seemed like this could have been true. After making further progress in French, though, I learned that Pierre was actually saying, *My pockets are so empty.*

Pierre's pockets are so empty. Pierre likes to bite his fingernails. Pierre speaks carefully and quietly. Pierre is a shop assistant at a bookstore. There, the physical capital of Pierre's ancestors clashes wordlessly with the economic capital of wealthy Asian tourists. The books are in conversation; the people are in conflict.

Shahin is a Sudanese refugee, his Facebook profile picture is a photo of Frantz Fanon. His timeline is full of poems he wrote in Arabic. I press the translate button to read them and it gives me back unintelligible text:

The inferiority complex of a chemical compound
We do nothing, we just rebel against our own image
#... #... #... #...
The roses must be given to the children in the camp
While he was doing drugs, the darling baby returned
Early breakfast, going to the Sorbonne in Paris to look for his
brother Africa
Dance has already become cartridge lead
The future became their black intelligence
Lacking impartiality in the numbers of black lions
War in the black belt
#!. #!. #!. #!. #!. #!. #!. #!. #!.
Language like a spear launched from the body of the world pierces the
wound of the sky

He had already turned and taken one dose of race
We became Black, it is dynamic, we turn toward blackness, it holds more
value than whiteness
#... #... #... #... #... #... #...
Because demons are not Black

The whole class of eighteen people collaborates on a short film. In the
film we recite our own poems. When we reach my part of the film, you
can clearly see that my facial features seem to collapse into flatness. No
mountains or valleys or wild dense dark forests, I am all alluvial deltas and
tiny rice paddies. Low self-esteem has nowhere to hide when the global
resolution is so high. Asia's great twenty-first-century vindication, which
began with economics then spread to politics and to the military, has failed
to reach the body. Asia has been well-off for over a century, and yet we
still see European beauty as beauty. Aesthetics still drags behind politics, the
military, economics. Maybe after two hundred years we will finally catch up.
After two hundred years, we'll all be dead. And Pierre and his girlfriend will
have their stereotypical names carved on their tomb: PIERRE AND MARIE.
She's Dutch and as tall as he is.
   In the short film, Pierre bites his nails.
   Shahin does not recite his own poetry.
   Shahin recites Valéry.
   My poem is beautiful.

In a moment of joy, I throw off my shirt and open the curtains. The Moroccan
man stands at the window across the way, just as he has before. The sun is
positioned such that when he faces me, he is light and I am shadow, he is
shadow and I am light. He's smoking, his chest is bared, and he's looking
straight at me. His beard is stitched with sunlight, the lines of it as sharp as a
ceramic knife. He steps out of an Islamic miniature to gaze at my Asian body,
and I pierce the glassy air to gaze at his North African body. Under my
window is a blossoming cherry tree. Under his window is a palm tree. Across
the courtyard garden, our bodies mirror each other.
   A map of the world lightly floats down over our neighborhood, aligning
with the complex in which we live. On this map, the flower garden between
us is our Europe.
   A while ago I read, on a French internet forum, an Asian user's pleas for
advice. He said he was only two inches long and didn't dare to even hold
a woman's hand, for fear those slender white hands would start exploring
and his secret would be broken, the meaning of his life smashed like an egg.
   His comments were met with a chorus of concern. Very few people
laughed at him, the clamor was largely made up of courteous inquiries.
A North African user wrote back and said he himself was nearly eight inches,
which had already caused some awkwardness, though two inches was

particularly small. He knew of some corrective surgeries that might help. There was another North African woman user who advocated vehemently for love. She insisted that love could cure all ills and was the medicine for everything. It was all so warm and convivial. What a great multiracial nation.

The man taps his cigarette ash, and then returns to a meditative stillness. The capillaries on my arm are as legible as scripture. When he gazes at my Asian body, what is he thinking?

But what is an Asian body exactly? The world's focus on the European body is already excessive, the grace bestowed on it so great, that an Asian body is drawn to its own extinction.

An Asian body faces the mirror, the mirror's surface scorches and burns, and there is no one in the mirror. Like a heavenly fire, the great colonization consumed the beauty of millions. Out of the ashes, a sinister and foreign spirit of beauty was resurrected. The Buddha and the demon and the mandala returned to us from the West, and from then on Asian people saw only their own transfigurations in the mirror, they no longer saw themselves.

The Asian body and Asia itself are both blurred. Asia is a product of Europe, Europe whose absolute blue borders were painted by Christianity. Asia was named by Europe: Ασία in Greek, Asia in Latin. Asia is defined by Europe: sharing a continental plate, it is anywhere Europe is not. Formerly, Asian people did not know they lived in Asia. Asian people said they lived in: the Nine Provinces of Yu Gong, the land of the rising sun, the eight wildernesses, the six boundaries, the three thousand worlds unbounded. Asian people said they were: people.

When Europe arrived, their gods framed the universe, their people framed Asia. Asia is everything that Europe is not. Asia is Europe's perfect inverse. Europe is homogeneous, Asia is heterogeneous. Asia holds every type and color of person—red, yellow, white, black, and the green of youth—as well as the five major religions of Confucianism, Taoism, Buddhism, Christianity, and Islam. Its kaleidoscopic aesthetics, later completely destroyed, flowed from the Caucasus Mountains all the way to the Japanese archipelago. And then the people of Asia were no longer people, they became an entity called Asians, a kind of humanoid the deep-eyed, peak-nosed ethnic group of the ancient northwest treated as a curiosity.

If you've never gone to Paris, you don't know that the best-selling item in the Carrefour stores is a factory-produced Buddha head, neatly cut off at the neck, made to be placed against window curtains or next to wineglasses. The Buddha is also an Asian person.

The Eastern body became a battlefield, magnetized toward the West. Impelled by aesthetics, each Asian body is forced to rise, to spin around, to regard itself, to distort itself, to falsify itself, and then to slouch toward the perfection of the West—that world of eternal bliss.

The celebrated cosmetic surgery in East Asia looks toward the West, instead of being guided by its own millennia of beauty. And so the people of the East have gradually come to resemble the people of the West, the aesthetics of the Eurasian continent stretching out in a ten-thousand-mile-long Möbius strip, and the distant foreign world becomes a distorted reflection of the homeland.

In Asia, I was not in the least aware of my body. Only after arriving in Europe did I discover that my body carried Asia within it. In Taiwan, a body might be seen as old, young, tall, short, fat, or thin; a body is not understood in terms of its geographical origin. In Paris, when I travel by subway, I am weighed down by other people's curiosity. It rides the shifting expressions in their eyes like currents, offers itself to me shyly, like a present. And it's as if, when they see me, I were the most beautiful bloom in Saint-Germain-des-Prés. I became self-conscious, I saw the watermark on my own body: my dark black pupils, my straight hair. I fell prey to the gazes of strangers that routed me out just as their forebearers had hunted and killed forest tribes to collect their skulls. On the Paris Métro, I define for 2.2 million pairs of European eyes the lands and people that their ancestors once claimed.

I thank them. I thank you. The Asian eye covets the European body, the European eye covets the Asian body. And in between these interweaving arrows, my self-awareness painfully yet joyfully carves itself into being.

I am here in this place, but my Asian body is absent. European people who stroll through museums catch sight of their own bodies, omnipresent and omnipotent, in mythic ascension, in golden robes and emperor crowns, in the habits of religious martyrs. One moment they may be an excavated Greek statue lifted from out of the ocean, the next they might become a member of the Protestant gentry in the Dutch Golden Age, necks encircled in stiff lace, and then, for a time, they might be a brutalist self-portrait composed of thick distinct brushstrokes. The European face in history changes and then changes again. The European body is represented and re-created in a thousand brilliant ways: realistic, abstract, in a crowd, as a portrait. After the great colonization, European art subsumed global art. White people saw themselves reenacted, celebrated in song, performed and interpreted on a global scale. The whole of art history is white people drawing their own history. They walk into a museum and walk into an imaginary reality, like a fantasy game. An Italian tough takes a selfie with a bronze sculpture of a Roman emperor. In front of the statue of David, the person helping me take a picture so resembles David he could be a replica. It's as if David's spirit were helping me take a picture with David's corporeal body. In front of me, behind me, all around me: it's all Davids. Viewing such an exhibition feeds their ego: I may be an ordinary person, but I merit the artistic commemoration of two millennia.

As for Black, sublime, glorious, and profound Black: it is a descent, a retreat, a background, it is a point of contrast, an underlying meaning. If an African body comes to the museum, he catches sight of his representation as Satan, as a savage, as half beast tamed by a white Jesus, as cargo, as enchanter, as a shadow, as a slave girl holding fresh flowers. The museum besieges the African body.

As for the Asian body, it is a zero, it is an absence, it has not existed since heaven and earth began. I steer my Asian body through the exhibition space the way a wheelchair-bound person trespasses into a lavish room with no accessibility—but in my case, even the wheelchair is empty. It seems as if I've arrived only to fill an empty space. No one asks me to leave, no one speaks to me. I am silent, I am transparent, their eyes cut right through me, they instead perceive a cocktail of everything Eastern. I feel a loss so vast it has lasted for a thousand years.

I finish reading my poem. But there is only silence, and the blankness of an empty sky that fills the small room of this theater on the outskirts of Paris. Seventeen people with seventeen different expressions in their eyes.

Inside this theater classroom, under the high-hanging costumes of past generations of Europeans, our several-month-long writing workshop draws to an end with my outburst.

Afterward, Pierre disagrees with me. He says, "It's not that complicated."

Shahin disagrees with me. He says, "It's not that simple."

I say, "Pierre, you know you hold an advantage, even though you choose not to acknowledge it. Or if you acknowledge it, you don't talk about the bitterness that comes with the sweetness."

I say, "Shahin, it's not difficult. I've noticed your beauty. Your Black beauty and your Sundanese-ness that outshine the white lens."

Shahin says, "You use European eyes to look at me. You're not praising my beauty. You're praising the fact that I happen to have an African body that aligns with European beauty standards. Do you know what the standards of African beauty are? Because by those standards, I am not beautiful at all. Did you know that using European beauty standards to judge African bodies has resulted in great suffering? On your Asian body is a pair of European eyes. You see me deformed and yourself distorted. The African body is fighting to pick off all these European eyes. As for the Asian body, when will it have Asian eyes?"

I steer my Asian body away from Pierre and Shahin.

In the gathering dusk, on Line 13 of the Métro, I am inlaid in the crowd, like a wisp of golden clay, like kintsugi.

Shahin publishes a new poem.

I press the translate button, but it won't translate, all I can understand is that the subject of the poem is the body.

The Arabic alphabet is strikingly beautiful in its blackness, the translate button flashes bright like my white eyes.

＊

After I exploded into an Oriental rainbow, my lover and I began to date. This man was the only person whose ethnicity I could not clearly identify.

But he was not blurry. He was as brilliant and relentless as a blade, not stopping until a bit of blood was drawn.

To reconstruct myself through my encounters with other bodies was like making a coin rubbing; by saying what I was not, I arrived at a definition of what I am. Unexpectedly, I found my Asian body celebrated along the way, its path strewn with lanterns, and banners, and songs. The beauty I had assumed I did not possess was brought to the surface.

The last time I orgasmed, I forgot to shut the curtains. The two of us melted into the futon, while, across the way, the Moroccan man rested against his window, like a mirror image, smoking a cigarette.

The following day was Paris Pride. The sunlight was like a knife. I hurriedly threw on some clothes and rushed outside. On the tree-lined boulevard, someone obstructed my path. It was the Moroccan man, my beloved mirror image, his beard as impenetrable as a thicket, on his cheek a tiny rainbow flag.

His body, like his country, was its borders and everything it contained. To his north, Pierre. To his south, Shahin. All that he possessed, I lacked, all that I possessed, he lacked. He told me, "You're beautiful." I didn't know whether he was speaking of me at that moment, or of the moment when I was completely spent in climax. I laughed loudly and said, "You're beautiful, too." I lightly kissed the Moroccan man. I cannot say I had no regrets.

In the turbulence of the throng, I caught sight of the man with the undefined ethnicity, the man whom my love defined. He smiled quietly and watched me in awe. He didn't see Paris, didn't see Asia, didn't see a body, he saw only me. ✦

COVER GROUND: URUGUAY

For much of the twentieth century, the history of graphic design has been written from a Euro-American perspective. In recent years, however, the internet has allowed for a recentering of the narrative. La Patria, an online archive of Uruguayan graphic design founded by typeface designer Gabriel Benderski, is one of many small, focused collections that showcase the discipline's lineage throughout the world.

While much of Central and South America has long been internationally recognized for its graphic heritages, Uruguay was not often included in the conversation. Over the past few years, though, Benderski has discovered and recovered an impressive legacy of vintage and contemporary design, revealing vivid examples of Uruguayan Modernism.

One of the premier cover designers in Patria's collection is Fernando Álvarez Cozzi. "His approach is characterized by a visual synthesis of a few elements that communicate the message," Benderski explains, "to which he adds naïveté—that is, artlessness—bright and contrasting colors, and the free interpretation of perspective, or even the absence of it."

Álvarez Cozzi follows the Cuban and Polish schools, which many Uruguayans encountered during the mid-'60s through the popular magazine *Poland*. These stylistic approaches are unique for their strong lines, illustrative imagery, and limited, bold colors. "Uruguayan designers are, for the most part, self-taught artists who come from the world of illustration," Benderski says. "They had to use their strengths to figure out how to design."

The limited resources caused by the 1973 coup and the ensuing twelve-year civic-military dictatorship made ink a rare commodity. Uruguayan designers routinely had to make do with the supplies and technologies available to them. In Uruguay, there is what Benderski calls "a particular way of working . . . Uruguayans design with what there is. In other places, [things are] designed with an abundance of resources. In Uruguay, that isn't the case. It is not that we are underprivileged—it's that the limitations are noticeable." In some countries a photographer, an illuminator, a couple of designers, and an art director would collaborate on an image, while in Uruguay, the job was — and still is—often done by a single person. "I don't see it as a disadvantage," Benderski says. "On the contrary, it is a great virtue that allows us to have control over all parts." ✦
—*Steven Heller*

Publisher: Arca
Design by Carlos Palleiro (1973)

Publisher: Librería Linardi y Risso
Design by Horacio Añón (1999)

Publisher: Calicanto
Design by Fernando Álvarez Cozzi (1979)

Publisher: Cámara Uruguaya del Libro
Design by Horacio Añón (1987)

Publisher: Arca
Design by Carlos Palleiro (1973)

Publisher: Arca
Design by Carlos Palleiro (1975)

Publisher: Arca
Design by Jorge Carrozzino & Nicolás Loureiro (1969)

Publisher: Ediciones de Uno
Design by Maca (1988)

AMORIM MIEL PARA LA LUNA · CERNO

Publisher: Cerno
Design by Rossi (1969)

Publisher: Ediciones de Uno
Design by Maca (1982)

Publisher: Banda Oriental
Design by Fernando Álvarez Cozzi (1976)

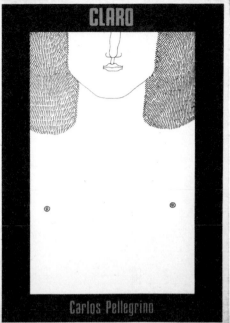

Publisher: Arca
Design by Carlos Palleiro (1977)

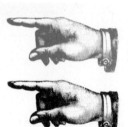

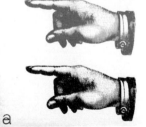

Publisher: Arca
Design by Jorge Carrozzino & Nicolás Loureiro (1969)

Publisher: Banda Oriental
Design by Fernando Álvarez Cozzi (1976)

Maja Haderlap
Translated from the GERMAN by TESS LEWIS

venezia
we sit on the pier of this fish-city,
which swings on the hook of the tide,
and cannot escape it. we talk about ourselves
and what holds us captive here
on the shore between north and south.
the mosaics of aquileia, i say,
the swaying dolphins and spiny lobster,
that found refuge in trees from the great flood.
the snow-crowned alps that surge skyward
like an ossified, wildly agitated sea.
the timavo's dark maw, you say,
out of which the river surges as if it were
flowing from one abyss into the next,
the houses in this city, like mussels
washed ashore, weather-beaten and rotting,
the algae spread like a carpet
at our feet. lines of words swim like lures
in the lagoons. we sit for the catch and laugh.
bubbles rise from our noses,
scales of stone fall from our eyes—
we are finally caught in this place's net.

happy in sveti ivan
as long as i remain stretched out
in the shadow of the apse,
a ribbon of meadow ants will flow
through my veins. arterial walls
will echo with their most delicate steps.
bee beetles will take off their shaggy
furs and nest in the hair on my nape.

an ortolan will land on my forehead
and peck the biscuit crumbs from my lips.
or i could rise and stroke your
flanks, pull you to the dry fountain,
to the playgrounds where counting rhymes
can be heard and the sweet hum
of small children's voices. i could also
drop off to sleep and fall upward
to the olive tree leaves, small wings could sprout
in my armpits, which you will glimpse
when i wave to you mid-flight.

on the shore path in the evening light
on which i stood one day,
at the end of a summer
that broke me open like a small
fruit (i was bitter and very tough)
—a mote of light falls on me
a spark from abiding time.

the impatiens still throws
its blossoms into the air like balls.
it tumbles down, sinks in the water
and disappears. a grain of light rises,
as it had back then and dies away.

the shore path is now built up, shifted,
torn out of the meadow and discarded.
i, too, have emerged repeatedly
as a translation of myself,
transferred and rewritten
i appear in a new transcription
although in a similar form.

the second of light takes flight,
the spark of a time that remains,
scatters, and returns.

MAN
MOUNTAIN

Catherine Lacey

ILLUSTRATION BY Moonassi

I CANNOT SAY I fully understood where it came from, but I think we all understood, in a way, where it came from. Not physically where it came from—I mean, no one could really explain that—but the mountain's sudden appearance was at least understandable from a metaphoric, philosophical, and/or emotional perspective, which is to say it made sense astrologically even if it did not make sense logically.

Logic and reason (remember reason?) had long ago fallen out of fashion. The calm among us—and there were still a few calm among us—kept saying there was no need to worry, that history was cyclical and we had simply entered a recurrent era of abject chaos. This was the "Goodnight Mush" part of the century, time for the chrysalis to turn soupy. This was the year a mountain spontaneously materialized in rural Kansas, one kilometer high, composed entirely of semiconscious adult men.

When I heard about the Man Mountain I was, of course, at the gym. Those of us who were not comforted by the historical view of the contemporary moment—a nagging sense of being prewar—had taken matters into our own hands in the only way we could—that is, symbolically—and began training for the figurative and literal wars that were both imminent and present. Most of the women I knew (though I only really knew or seemed to know the people who also spent most of their waking hours at the gym) kept strict training schedules in Muay Thai, jujitsu, boxing, or semi-acrobatic styles of weightlifting. In an era of perpetual crisis, we soothed ourselves by caring inordinately about how tall a box we could jump onto, or how much we could deadlift, or how many times we could flip a truck tire. In idle moments, we imagined perfecting the form of our pull-ups, our push-ups, our jabs and jump squats, and we pitied the women who still did yoga, except the ones who did that torturous heated variety with their tongues sticking out, contorted and menacing and psycho-spiritually weaponized. They were alright—mostly—though we felt they had not yet realized that inner peace was a patricapitalist fantasy and the only reasonable thing a woman could do now was amass an anti-estrogenic cluster of meat around her controversial guts and train for battle.

"Our Bodies, Our Machines," we said. There was no time for softness. There was no time for time. Sometimes, between sets, we would look at each other and just say what year it was—could you believe it? And no one could believe it—then we would return with new hostility to our routines, laboring until we were sweating blood, spitting blood, until blood soaked our hair and slicked our limbs, until blood issued from our every pore and pit.

So when news broke about the Man Mountain I just thought, Uh, what? Then, like so many unbelievable things, it became completely believable, and all there was left to do was to climb it.

Not to blow my own horn (but also not to apologize for blowing my own horn because what else are you supposed to do with your own horn) but I probably ranked in the top tier of nominally amateur American athletes most prepared to conquer the Man Mountain. I don't know how you could have polled for that, but I feel confident that it was, and still is, true. I'd spent a lot of time at my local climbing gym, then a few other climbing gyms, then I went rogue and started climbing straight up buildings, trees, gates, traffic lights, anything. Maybe I didn't have time to eat solid food anymore and maybe I wasn't being an effective employee and perhaps I didn't have an actual human-on-human relationship in my day-to-day, but none of that mattered anymore because I was no longer exactly human, but something closer to a spider—spindly and silent and menacing, frightening nice people as I hoisted myself onto their balconies.

So I drove straight to Kansas and, uh, *whoa*. The pictures and the videos and the three-dimensional animated renderings of the Man Mountain did not really convey the thingness of this thing. It was a real stumper. It was, I don't know, a feat? But whose feat? A feat of what? Several television trucks were there, but none of the reporters could look away for long enough to read their teleprompters. Policemen and National Guards and SWAT teams idled in dark hordes, but there seemed to be no agreement about how to proceed—which way to point the guns, whether it was a crime scene or not, whether the Man Mountain needed protection from the people or whether it was the other way around. Some UFO enthusiasts had gathered, smug and reverent, and there were several varieties of cult members and leaders, many forms of clergy, druids, leftover Y2Kers, a few seemingly unaffiliated drum circles, and so on. Each of them claimed the mountain as confirmation of whatever they needed confirmed; it had been prophesied, and now was a time for great rejoicing and repentance and sudden death. They looked up at the large Kansas sky, gleeful and reassured.

I stood away from the crowd. An expectant solitude washed over me as I contemplated the possibly sinister and as yet unknown force(s) that could have created the Man Mountain, and my understanding of the basic foundation of reality shifted beneath my feet. It was reassuring, at least, that something literal and serious had occurred in this time of chronic indifference and rumor. The Man Mountain was not contingent or theoretical. It was not a think piece. It was here and large and undeniable. The few who attempted to take photographs of the Man Mountain all failed, as the feeling of being in its presence resisted digitization. It was the only event for many years that lacked an obvious political narrative or conspiracy or apocrypha.

The base was exceptionally easy to scale, almost as if it had been designed this way. Holds were plentiful and well spaced. I grabbed a foot, an elbow. Thighs and buttocks gave gently beneath my feet. Up close, none of the men seemed to be asleep, exactly, yet none were quite awake. Most of their eyes were shut or fluttering, and all of them held slight grins, as if they understood and accepted the strange enormity of their predicament. Every limb I held as I scaled seemed to teem with itself, forcefully occupying its place in the pile. There was no passivity here, no victimization. The Man Mountain was, I inferred, a wonder of sheer will.

About thirty feet up I came across Justin.

Justin? What are you doing here? Whoa! Justin!

His eyes shocked open like a corpse in a horror film, which would have startled me if I hadn't been engaged in military-grade stress training for several years. Justin began to move his mouth, the muscles as loose and uncontrolled as an infant's.

Hey.

Yeah, I said. *Hey.*

A broad man sandwiched sideways in the mountain created a ledge I rested on to talk to Justin.

It's been a while, I said.

Yeah, he said.

Are you alright? Do you want me to, uh, help get you out of here or . . . ?

Nah.

Cool. Okay. Well. Maybe I'll see you around?

Justin didn't reply so I kept on moving upward, but what did I even mean: *Maybe I'll see you around?* Around what? Around when? Recently my emails had started writing themselves—I would click to open a reply, then the computer would just take over and words appeared on the screen, words I recognized as unremarkably my own. Even our emails knew, for absolute certain, that no one had said anything unpredictable in many years.

And when, exactly, had I even met Justin? I couldn't remember if he was someone to whom I'd given my vague approval or whether he was someone I suspected capable of performing the acts of evil so casually enjoyed by those with disposable incomes and frictionless societal existences. I was pretty sure we'd met at a party hosted in a town house owned and renovated by a tech start-up. A large fiberglass horse took up much of one living room. It seemed several young men lived there, and several maids would appear and clean it when one of those young men summoned them through one of the apps that had been developed by the start-up they'd started. A grove's worth of potted fig trees filled the rooms, all of them well cared for, some of them fruiting. One room was arranged with sofas and armchairs that looked like the cartoonish, inflatable furniture sold in late-nineties American malls, only this furniture did not deflate. These chairs, you had to live with them.

Justin had been playing a vintage pinball machine under a black crystal chandelier while explaining some complex opinion to another man, or maybe Justin was the one listening instead of speaking or maybe Justin and I observed these two men by the pinball machine or perhaps Justin was someone else entirely. It's difficult for me to remember, as this was a very long time ago, at least one presidential era into the past. In fact, Justin may not have been either of those men but instead the one who had either invited or escorted me to the tech town house, and if that is the case then I am even less sure about how I first came across Justin and now that I think of it I am less sure about his name being Justin, or—another likely case—half or more of the men in that town house were named Justin. At the time I thought an important part of being a human was appearing before other humans and demonstrating the facts of your humanity—your name, age, origin, collegiate affiliations, career, ambitions, social standing, and whether you slept in a bed with another person and if so what sort of genitalia that person had and if not what sort of genitalia you would accept on the body of a person with whom you might consider sharing a bed.

But then I joined a gym and realized that it is totally possible to commit to a life lived primarily within one's legal, corporeal limits, and of pushing one's living corpse to the outskirts of its abilities, of measuring out the finite weeks in leg, arm, back, or ab days, of monitoring the fluctuations of a body fat percentage, of scrupulously observing the material intake and output of one's body, of tracking the incremental progress of how well one is able to pick something up and put it down again. There was nothing, it sometimes seemed, that I couldn't lift and set down again, nothing I couldn't climb, nothing I couldn't put below me.

Anyway, I soon realized my ascent of the Man Mountain was going a little too easily—it just wasn't the challenge I'd been hoping for as I wasted all those hours driving to Kansas. In boredom, I stopped on a man situated horizontally in the pile much like the man I'd perched upon to talk to Justin, and in fact this man looked so much like that last man that it might have been the same man and turning to my right I found, again, Justin's face, his eyes just as wide as before.

Hey, Justin 2 said, but I could not bring myself to reply. Had I somehow climbed in a circle? I had, I thought, been climbing straight up. I looked down at the spectators and SWAT teams and television trucks below; everyone was still staring up or moving around haphazardly, pacing, confused, aimless. I leaned back against the chest of a man in a pale green polo shirt. *Hey,* Justin 2 said again, but I didn't have any ability or desire to speak to Justin 2 for the first or second time. Something was not right. Something, maybe, was very wrong.

A foot jutted out right next to my head—it wore a polished leather shoe and a sock patterned with little red and blue birds flying to and from and with and against one another. The ankle of this foot seemed to be in good condition, probably had a decent bone density, healthy ligaments. I'd once seen someone drop a sixty-pound metal orb on his bare foot and as the orb rolled off, his foot seemed smaller than ever, but by the time the ambulance came the foot had swollen to the size of a small head. The guy on the other end of that foot was stuck in bed for months, losing all his life's gains, all his strength evaporating in his inaction. To get out of bed he needed permission from both his feet and one of them would simply no longer give it. His foot, it seemed, could not forgive him.

And what part of my body would someday not forgive me? I often succeeded in never thinking of such things by thinking instead of inputs and outputs, measures and reps, by focusing on progress and never on ends. But here on this heap of men, everything seemed closer than ever to ending, and all at once I was engulfed by a great arbitrary vortex that goes by the name of God.

All those heights I had climbed, all my strength, all my effort and torn muscle rebuilt and rebuilt, not even God could see it, and I knew that then, or I felt that I knew it, or maybe I just felt a breeze and knew it to be the cool and apathetic gaze of God. I was in a race against my own potential weakness and I was winning and I was losing.

Hey! Justin 2 said again.

No, I thought, that's quite enough. I simply cannot tolerate being so social anymore, not today, not in this crisis. There were just too many people in this Man Mountain, and I had not come here to make friends—I had come here to climb! Well! I wasn't going to waste my little time any more. I started scaling down the Man Mountain, which is always awkward-looking and never quite as easy as going up. I passed the initial Justin, who calmly watched my descent, but then I passed Justin again, and though I quickened my pace, I passed yet another Justin or perhaps the same Justin and when I looked down to estimate how close the ground was, it seemed I hadn't moved any closer to the base of the mountain.

Then, as if this world had spontaneously begun to understand my trouble, a rope ladder dropped from a helicopter. I leaped to and ascended it, and how strange it was to realize that climbing something as unusual as a pile of men could be so boring while climbing something as unremarkable as a rope could be so thrilling. The wind whipped up by the helicopter blades rushed through my four actual and my four invisible limbs and for a few moments everything I'd ever done seemed worth the hassle. God could take me or leave me.

In the helicopter several reporters were huddled, and one of them had a large microphone she held to my mouth as she shouted questions over the helicopter's nearly deafening whir: What were the Men of the Man Mountain like and what were they doing there in a pile like that and what did I think it meant and did I think the federal government should intervene or should they leave it up to the state of Kansas and what would I like to tell the American People and did any of the Men in the Mountain say anything to me and did I say anything to them and did I suspect foul play or divinity and, yes, most importantly, did I think the Man Mountain was an Act of God?

I wanted to answer the reporter, but I didn't want to answer her questions. I shook my head, so she re-shouted her questions, all of them the same, just louder, meaner. How could she have known that I, a human spider, can hear very precisely through both my ears and the extremely tiny and biologically complex hairs that cover my body and limbs? She couldn't have known. The truth is that spiders and humans know very little about one another, and human spiders know even less about themselves. I tried to answer her questions, but my ears were bleeding. I'm simply too sensitive. I just want to climb on everything, keep climbing on everything up and always up, to reach the top or die trying. I tried to speak; I may have spoken. Perhaps I should have kept quiet. Below us everyone kept struggling and failing to know how the world had come to this, and above us no one even bothered to ask the question. ✦

FOUR POEMS
Rachel Mannheimer

THE MOON

I'd never experienced virtual reality,
nor, I soon felt, had I ever experienced anything
so dazzling and hateful at once. The VR installation was called
To the Moon. It accommodated two
museum visitors at a time, and I'd made the appointment
so we could go together.
With my headset in place, the room was still there
but my body disappeared. The stool where Chris had sat beside me
was there, but Chris was gone. Then the room was gone
and I was alone on the moon. The feeling of transport was real
and the feeling of space—

But the attendant had promised flying—*just extend your arms*—
and it didn't feel like flying. It felt, crushingly, like I was missing out
on a major part of the moon experience.
There were ghostly dinosaurs on the moon,
there was a giant solitary rose made out of moon rock and a donkey
that I rode along the surface of the moon.
I came to the edge of a crater and wanted to jump
but this was a passive section of the experience.
What did you see on the moon? I demanded as we left,
but Chris was experiencing nausea. He'd had a bad cold that week
so I'd been thinking about his death—
and now the aftershock
of my abandonment on the moon left me weeping.

What did you see on the moon? The attendant went in behind us
to wipe down the headsets, to welcome the next guests. I was angry

because this all felt like a vision of the future.
But maybe that's how people felt
when we landed on the moon.

Chris and I had both been granted residencies at the museum
for our writing, impossible luck,
and over the days had freely walked
through galleries that required no appointment.
But with Chris's illness, we'd been sleeping
in separate rooms, then going to our separate studios,
and now our separate moons—Chris flying and swooping
so dramatically you could vomit, while I stayed down on the ground.

That's how it was, sometimes, living with another poet.
Like we could both put on headsets and wave the controllers—
arms outstretched and triggers depressed—but for me alone
nothing happened. People say that poets love the moon,
but I got into poetry because I liked words and small things
and lacked the imagination for fiction.

There's a book my dad would read us
about a princess who falls ill and won't be well until they bring the moon,
it's hopeless! But then someone asks
what she thinks the moon might be:
a disc of gold, no bigger than her thumbnail.
So, then, quite achievable.
But what will happen when, moon in hand, she sees the moon
still in the sky? It's fine—in her cosmology,
the moon grows back like a tooth. The book is called *Many Moons*.
Outside my studio window, dirty snow is piled up
around a pool of ice. When I arrived, it was liquid,
but it will be an ice rink soon—
I've seen them work, they hose it down to smooth it.
Now it's night. Two men climb into cars on either side, their headlights
meet across the ice. Now two visitors approach on foot.
Tenderly, and not with their full weight—with one foot each—they test the ice.
The moon is far away for all to see. I'm imagining the poems Chris will write.

NEW YORK

Arizona was the first dance made by Robert Morris, 1963 at Judson Memorial Church. The dance was twenty minutes long, in four sections, accompanied in part by a recording of the artist reading his text "A Method for Sorting Cows." *Two men are required to sort cows in the method presented here.* It was a solo performance.

For the second section, Morris stood at center stage beside a T-like form, which he repeatedly adjusted and retreated from. A lampstand, two sticks. Morris had developed an interest in dance having married the dancer Simone Forti.

(He later left the field at the behest of dancer Yvonne Rainer.)

In 1961 or 2 (sources vary), he'd staged a performance, part of an evening organized by La Monte Young at the Living Theatre. A sculpture he'd built—a plywood rectangular column, *Column*—"performed" a choreography. For three and a half minutes, it stood upright, then it toppled and lay on stage for another three and a half. Morris, in the wings, knocked the column over by pulling an invisible string. Initially, the idea had been for him to stand inside the column and effectuate the fall, but rehearsing the maneuver in Yoko Ono's loft, he'd gashed his eyebrow and ended up in the ER.

Forti had put on a program in that same loft in '61, involving movement, objects, and rules. For one piece, in which Morris participated with artist Robert Huot, she'd installed two heavy screw eyes in the wall. Morris was instructed to lie on the floor and stay there at all costs; Huot, given an eight-foot rope, was instructed to tie him to the wall.

In New York, I'd had an affair with a man who volunteered at the *Dream House*, the sound and light environment created by La Monte Young and his wife, Marian Zazeela. Basically, Young designed the droning sound and Zazeela the magenta light. It was installed in a loft downtown. The man I knew was in charge of asking visitors to remove their shoes, and watched over their stuff while they were inside. When I went to see him there, I realized how much his own apartment—which he kept dim, with colored bulbs, and where he played obscure records—was inspired by this place. I did feel, in his apartment, like I was in an altered state. A couple times, I cat-sat for him, and the place was mine. He never saw where I lived.

Because we mostly met for sex, and because his apartment was small, and mostly bed, it felt, sometimes, like a stage for sex. Also, the sex was more prop-based than I was accustomed to—ropes and gags. I stayed naked, and he drew me baths and adored my flesh and I barely talked and felt like a cat, or a five-foot tower of fruit.

The critic Michael Fried, in his essay "Art and Objecthood" in *Artforum*, dismissed the "literalist" sculptures of Robert Morris and Donald Judd as "fundamentally theatrical." He quotes from Morris's own *Artforum* essay "Notes on Sculpture":

One's awareness of oneself existing in the same space as the work is stronger than in previous work, with its many internal relationships. One is more aware than before that he himself is establishing relationships as he apprehends the object from various positions and under varying conditions of light and spatial context.

Fried takes this and argues that literalist art, like theater, exists for an audience. You might say the art is activated by the beholder, who encounters—within this staged environment, under these lights, etc.–a *situation*. But what Morris describes isn't viewer as audience. Both viewer and object are dancers.

NEW YORK

After he moved to Seattle,
I couldn't get any other man
to do it right.
No, not like you're mad at me.

THE MOON

Bausch had her dancers create movements
to express ideas, experiences.
"The moon?" I depicted the word with my body
so she could see and feel it.

For *Vollmond*, a giant chunk
of rock evokes a lunar landscape.
Water fills a wide, shallow trough in the stage,
reflecting the dancers' movements.
Rain falls intermittently.

Dancers climb the rock. Dancers climb
other dancers. Rain falls and men with poles
sort of row themselves across the stage,
skate-sliding on the surface.
Now they swim-slide on their bellies
in the overflowing trough.

I watched this, finally, in *Pina*, the movie,
while Chris listened to something
in the other room.

Dancers wade into the trough,
scoop water up in buckets
and splash it on the giant rock,
like trying to save a whale.
They throw water on each other,
on themselves, their clothes are drenched.
The water stuff is primal. There are other
heterosexual antics, too, not in the film.
A man races against the clock to undo
a woman's bra. Men pour liquid
from bottles from great heights,
overfilling women's glasses.

Vollmond was one of Pina's last works.
Of the performances after her death, critics expressed
a certain weariness, alongside great esteem.
Nothing remains new.

She requested a gesture related to "joy"—
joy or the pleasure of moving.
From the movement I presented,
she created an entire scene.

ROLE PLAY
Maria Clara Drummond
Translated from the PORTUGUESE by ZOË PERRY

I'M A MISOGYNIST and a misandrist. I have zero patience for men or women, nothing against them, I just don't enjoy interacting. I've got nothing to say, I feel like I'm being condescending the whole time, or they're being condescending to me. But I'm not a complete misanthrope, because I do like gay men. They're the only kind of human beings who are actually capable of coexisting on an equal footing. I don't feel comfortable in the milieu assigned to me at birth. Just the thought of marriage and kids makes me want to gag. I could list all the reasons why, but it would sound silly and dated, and above all, it might make me sound like one of those fag hags who wants her very own gay bestie. Get with the program. Gays are for life, not just for Christmas. To make sure it's perfectly clear that I'm not one of those women, I like to slip in some queer slang, a word or two in Pajubá, preferably intermediate level, because even my mother knows the basics, and using more advanced vocabulary sounds like you're trying too hard. Or I'll decide to tell some revealing story, like about the time two guy friends of mine met each other in one of the dark rooms in Berghain. "You're Vivian's friend, aren't you?" one of them asked the other, while they were going at it. It's good to belong to a group. Anyway, I have to rein in my anxiety, and not just let encrypted codes fly rapid fire, because people who belong are chill, they don't try to send any signals, because they feel at home, and what I really want is to feel at home.

For a long time, I lived between Rio and São Paulo, depending on my job. Sometimes the jobs were longer-term, sometimes they were temporary, but they were always erratic, unstable, and underpaid, if paid at all. Still, I stuck with them because each one meant bonus points on my résumé. I'm an independent curator, I've worked in galleries, biennials, museums, ateliers, I've assisted on large exhibitions, I've produced smaller but significant shows on my own, I write art criticism for magazines and newspapers, both here and abroad. Then people congratulate me, my parents give me things like a trip to Berlin, a Comme des Garçons wallet, a Francesca Woodman photograph. I don't work with painters or photographers because they're straight. Sometimes shit gets messy, some of them are charming, with an artist's self-confidence. Next thing I know, I'm having sex with the guy at his opening, locked in the gallery bathroom, then I'm sharing a line left over from the night before at 11 A.M. on a Saturday. In the end, they always come away even more self-assured and I almost never orgasm. That's why I prefer other types of artists, who, while still narcissistic, are at least fun, and talk to me as an equal, with zero risk of emotional entanglement.

Around my thirtieth birthday, my parents bought me an apartment in Botafogo: two bedrooms, hardwood floors, ninety square meters, twenty-four-hour doorman. As a bonus, they also lent me a Sergio Rodrigues Mole armchair (the dog had chewed up some of the leather, they said they would take it back when they found a good upholsterer, but that was two years ago now, I think they've forgotten). It looked nice next to my massive João Silva photograph. It was a gift—I mean, I paid for the printing and framing, but now my place has another work of art, from the same series that's at MALBA.

This period coincided with a major upgrade to my résumé. I started exclusively taking jobs that would help my career, without considering finances. And if things got tight, whatever that meant, I'd rent out my apartment for two or three weeks and spend some time at my family's spare apartment in São Paulo. This system was especially profitable during Carnaval and on New Year's Eve. I'd earn enough money to last a few months, take some time off for a vacation, go abroad, who knows, maybe get a little Botox.

The location was perfect, street vendors were out seven days a week, all night long, always well stocked with Heineken. Darlene, who used to set up right in front of my building, warned me it was dangerous on the other side of the street, that there had been an execution-style shooting, nasty stuff. I wasn't worried, she might just have been trying to squash the competition. The joys of homeownership are many. I got to choose the color of the bedroom wallpaper, I made a spacious closet out of the old maid's room, and I had a kitchen that opened onto the living room, with soundproof windows. I wanted to leave the bathroom almost identical to the original because I like that fifties middle-class aesthetic. "I don't understand this world of yours where apartments just appear out of nowhere," said Marina Falcão. Every week we'd throw a little party, I'd provide the fridge, the ice, the speakers, the red light bulb, and everybody would bring their own drinks, drugs, playlists. Sometimes the neighbors, all elderly, would complain, which was no big deal. Alex used to say, "They'll be dead soon, or gentrified out of here." Alex was in charge of bringing along the new generation of alternative nightlife queers, proud of their small subversive acts, like colorful earrings, pink nail polish, maybe a distinctly feminine outfit. They made the cast of characters more diverse, enriched the surroundings.

That day, I'd planned a dinner party here at home for my closest friends, and then we would head out, to a rave Rodrigo was DJing. I was so happy he'd come out of the closet, including to his family, who are even more conservative than mine, and who'd had high hopes we'd marry each other.

A few years ago, he even proposed we have a sham marriage so his parents would leave him alone. To top it off, we'd get a kick-ass reception and access to his place in Paris. The possibility of a conventional heteronormative life did sound tempting for about fifteen minutes, but then, not so much. In my opinion, Rodrigo should ditch his friends from school, those morons who work in finance, and meet more people who work in the art world.

Since Rodrigo would be the last to go on, not until morning, we left the apartment late, around two. This rave wouldn't be at some hellhole, with lasers, strobe lights, projectors. It was free entry, in the square, near the Banco do Brasil Cultural Center. The square was kind of like a public courtyard, so there was only one entrance, with a barricade and two security guards to control the crowd, hand out wristbands, watch out for possible incidents. It was a specific niche: the mostly white, wealthy, gay crowd who align themselves with liberal and progressive, but not necessarily leftist, values, at least in economic terms. As usual, street vendors peddled drinks while people waited to join the party.

To my surprise, Darlene, the woman who worked my street, was there, no longer selling beer, but caipirinhas. Beside her was a grumpy old man selling Heinekens. I waved at her, smiling, and yelled, "Hey!" João Silva left his place in line to go give her a hug, kiss her on the cheek, ask about her son. He could do this sort of thing without sounding condescending, but I could not. That's why I preferred to be more discreet, maintain a more professional relationship, customer and vendor, so that I didn't make some faux pas. Also, I hadn't even realized that on Saturdays, she was someone else, somewhere else, because in my mind she worked in front of my building every day. And I didn't know a thing about Darlene's family. The line moved along a few meters, and soon we were all stopped alongside her portable caipirinha stand. "I thought I might see you here!" João Silva said. João Silva lived in São Paulo, so how did he know Darlene's professional itinerary? All that from the handful of times he'd gone down to buy beer during parties at my place? Darlene, it turned out, was smart, quick, funny, well informed, even cultured. She spoke our language, she wasn't evangelical, and she voted for PSOL, which brought out a calm, fatherly expression on João Silva's face, and I think on mine, too. The conversation was so nice that no one noticed the sudden arrival of the municipal police.

The municipal police had always been a harmless bunch, but at that juncture in Brazilian politics things had started to get weird. The paddy wagon that pulled up in front of us looked like a SWAT vehicle, like the ones used by BOPE, the tactical operations squad. Five men, chests puffed out, stood facing the line. They gave off a hostility that was underscored by their larger-than-normal billy clubs. First, they approached the grumpy old man and took all his beer, put everything in the back of the van. "Hey, this is robbery!" shouted Marina Falcão, and the rest of the line agreed, booing so loud they drowned out the Italo disco tunes. This didn't embarrass the police. On the contrary, it stirred things up even more, and they charged at Darlene. Her cocktail supplies were destroyed, along with her bottles of cachaça, which were smashed on the ground. Darlene screamed and tried to break free from the man holding her arm, and in retaliation, she was slugged with a billy club. When Alex tried to intervene, inserting his body with its earrings, painted nails, and purple eye shadow, he was also beaten over the leg and the arm, and when he tried to retreat, he got hit in the ribs. He wasn't the only partygoer to take a stand, but the beatings were directed only at him. In the middle of the melee, a tear gas canister was tossed at the feet of those waiting in line, just a few feet away from the municipal police.

The rave's security guards ushered everyone inside in a hurry. Only the vendors were left outside. This may have been a protection tactic—perhaps the police were too intimidated to enter an upper-class party. But it didn't even cross our minds that the street vendors could enter that space as partygoers. In theory, the rave was free to all, and there was no practical reason for them not to come inside with us, especially because at that point, all their booze had already been confiscated. But there was a mutual, silent understanding that they didn't belong, and that was final.

Alex went home, slightly injured, and the rest of us, lulled by the acid that was starting to kick in, stayed at the party. "Forget about it, Vivian," said Marina Falcão. But as soon as we got inside, I realized something serious was going on outside. The crowd-control barricades—along with my poor eyesight, made even worse by the tear gas—blotted out the view. A block away, on the other corner, there was a twisted figure walking with difficulty, and I got the impression it might be Darlene. Had she been beaten with extra violence during those ten minutes of confusion when everyone—I mean us, the usual crowd—had entered the square? If it wasn't her, who else could it be? A beggar, a street kid, a crackhead? Maybe. Ten minutes is more than enough time to beat the hell out of someone. But if that's what happened, surely someone in line would have done something, called it out, protested. Surely they wouldn't have just followed in my footsteps, drawn toward the disco beats. ✦

 This is the first chapter of *Role Play* (*Os Coadjuvantes*) by Maria Clara Drummond, a novel in which the bubble of a narcissistic and privileged young woman from Rio de Janeiro's cultural elite is pierced in a moment of violence. Forthcoming in Brazil from Companhia das Letras in April, you can read the second chapter in translation on our website: www.astra-mag.com.

Fragments From "SILENT MECHANISMS"
Marcelo Morales
Translated from the SPANISH by KRISTIN DYKSTRA

On the sand there was an *aguamala*, jellyfish they call it in English, a fish made of gelatin. I remembered a poem by Tranströmer[1] where he writes about the meaning of words he scrawls in his notebook, half-asleep. When he wakes in the morning, the words lose their meaning, because there are things that like the jellyfish hold meaning only in their element. Outside it, the words were like medusae in sand . . .

"Marcelo, poke it. Isn't it just seaweed?"

As I prodded the gelatin fish with a stick, I remembered having lived something similar, an old love, in another country, on another beach.

In contrast to the poem, that love radiated significance beyond its element. As much as I want to deny it, my life happens through poetry, I explain the world to myself this way.

Loves that you carry inside always, as though they were imprisoned, like a DNA strand, like water inside a gelatin fish. Things without which life would have no meaning, things not solid yet strong.

"Poke it," she said, "Isn't it seaweed?"

"It looks like a membrane. The rest is air, only air."

＋

They say to a sick man, You're fine, you're fine. And still he's dying. I clear the coffee table after breakfast. One book called *Bright*, another book by Sally Mann. Today I had an idea while driving, something about love, happiness, and the void; but not so boring or trite, something really new. Something showing itself for the first time in years. Craters opening in Siberia due to global warming. Ice disappears, they appear: the bones, furs, methane, permafrost. I took a gray body from a sardine tin, read lines written by a friend, bad ones. Lines like: *if poetry doesn't save you within your lifetime, do not expect salvation.*

Your entire life lies behind. There's some moment when you don't make a full comeback, and aging begins. At dawn I open my eyes. The wireless phone, uncharged, is trying to communicate. It emits a sound . . .
I open the patio door. On top of the washer, the old electrical resistor from the Ocean heater.
Life doesn't seem extraordinary, just because it is.
The ocean, moving in the night.
A bomb that doesn't explode. An imaginary bomb, a real form of pressure. It is, basically, I think, the passage of time. It is, basically, I think, the rotation
of the earth.

Red chairs consisting of broken plastic. Pale light from the television, dust under the bed, car inside the garage, a motorcycle covered with a sheet, the blind closet moth on the curtain. Everything is fine. Like a perfect language, the mechanism, silent.

My heart thumps. We're surrounded. Response brigades and police officers. They shut the electricity off. In front of the Ministry of Culture, young people are singing. Earlier this afternoon, in the same place, they were reading poetry. Something is wrong when that which is poetic becomes subversive. Power can be cold. Those of us who are older know that. Faces light up over cell phones, a sea of lights. Poetry, who said it was innocuous? Anguish. This must be collateral beauty. You go as far as the fear allows.

She is innocent, the little girl is innocent. Outside: politics, hunger strike, repression, simulation and dissidence. The dance of ego. The girl is innocent, she should stay that way. A hummingbird flew rapidly across the room. The girl is innocent, she doesn't know fear. She should stay that way.

The soldiers in the street are silent, now they wear black. On television they're talking about a soft coup d'état, about imperialism and the CIA, acts of financial sabotage out of Miami, the same old machinery. *Within the revolution all rights, outside the revolution, no rights.* In front of the ministry, they were reading Vallejo, singing Silvio and Santiago, they were singing Serrat. There are things that you have to understand; for example, the center is minuscule in relation to everything else; for example, beauty happens off to the side, when ugliness holds the center.

1 "If you take them out of the water their entire form / disappears, like when / an unspeakable truth is lifted up out of the silence." "You might wake up during the night / and quickly throw some words down / on the nearest paper […] / (the words radiant with meaning!) but in the morning: the same words don't say anything." Tomas Tranströmer, from "Baltics"

A SUMMER NIGHT'S KISS
Sayaka Murata

Translated from the JAPANESE by GINNY TAPLEY TAKEMORI
ILLUSTRATION BY Ella May

SUMMER IS THE *season for kissing.* That's what her friend Kikue used to say, Yoshiko suddenly remembered as she took in the strong fragrance of the summer's night through the screen door.

Yoshiko had just turned seventy-five. She had never had sex and hadn't kissed anyone either. She had never even once had intercourse with her older husband, who had died five years earlier. Both of their daughters had been conceived by artificial insemination, and she was still a virgin when she became a mother. Both daughters were now married, and she was thoroughly enjoying living alone in the house her husband had left to her.

In all other respects she had lived an absolutely normal life, marrying, having a family, and getting old. Even so, the moment she let drop in some conversation or other that "I have never had that experience, you see," she would get a shocked reaction: "What? Why? I mean, what about your children? Eh? Artificial insemination? Why on earth would you do that?" Everyone would start nosily inquiring into the details of Yoshiko's sexual orientation and sex life, and ultimately she got fed up with this and made sure to keep quiet about it. When she said nothing, everyone treated her as an ordinary person. Yoshiko thought this kind of response from people was shallow, cruel, and arrogant.

She was just thinking it was about time to run her bath when her cell phone rang.

It was Kikue, who lived nearby.

"Hello, it's me," she said. "Won't you come over tonight? My little sister just sent me a box of peaches, and I don't know what to do with them. You were good at making that stuff, weren't you? You know, that boiled fruit thing."

"Compote?"

"That's the stuff. Come and make some. I get off work at ten, so come and meet me at the store. About an hour from now, okay?"

"Come on, you're not trying to take an elderly woman for a night stroll, are you? Not that I mind, though."

She'd come to know Kikue, who was the same age as she was, in a club at the local community center. Kikue had this wayward side to her that Yoshiko didn't dislike. She had remained single her whole life, and after retiring from her job she'd been living off her pension and the wages from her part-time job at the local convenience store. Yoshiko had been taken aback by her working a night shift where she had to briskly carry around heavy cardboard boxes, but Kikue coolly boasted, "I grew up on a farm, so this is nothing. It just takes a kind of discipline."

Yoshiko walked through the residential area to the store where Kikue worked, arriving just as Kikue was leaving.

"Don't you have a date tonight?" Yoshiko asked teasingly.

"Don't be silly. I go on dates only when it's raining. Nights as pleasant as this feel too wholesome for kissing on the street," Kikue replied primly.

Kikue had never experienced marriage, but she loved sex, and even now she was always chatting up men in the store, and she often went to bed with boys forty or fifty years younger than herself. She bragged about how even the manager was scared of her, calling her a nymphomaniac.

The two elderly women walked along the dark street together. In this residential area at night, with hardly a soul in sight, the noise of traffic echoed like the sound of waves.

Kikue took something out of the convenience store bag she was carrying. "Would you like one of these?" It was a plastic package of sweet warabimochi dumplings. "They were near the sell-by date and about to be thrown out, so I bought them. They're nicely chilled and delicious."

As they walked, Kikue poured some molasses syrup over the dumplings and put one in her mouth.

"You know, warabimochi resemble a boy's tongue. That's why I wanted to eat them. I feel like I'm kissing someone."

"Really? Well, I don't want one then," Yoshiko said, and shrugged.

"Oh dear, I shouldn't have said that." Kikue laughed.

Despite being polar opposites, they really were very alike. When Yoshiko had confessed that she was a virgin, all Kikue said was, "Really?"

"Well, just one then," Yoshiko said, taking one. Putting it to her mouth, she tore off a soft lump with her teeth and felt a rush of satisfaction.

"Such a passionate kiss!" Kikue laughed again, and their footsteps rang out brightly in the hushed night streets. ✦

Evan M. Cohen

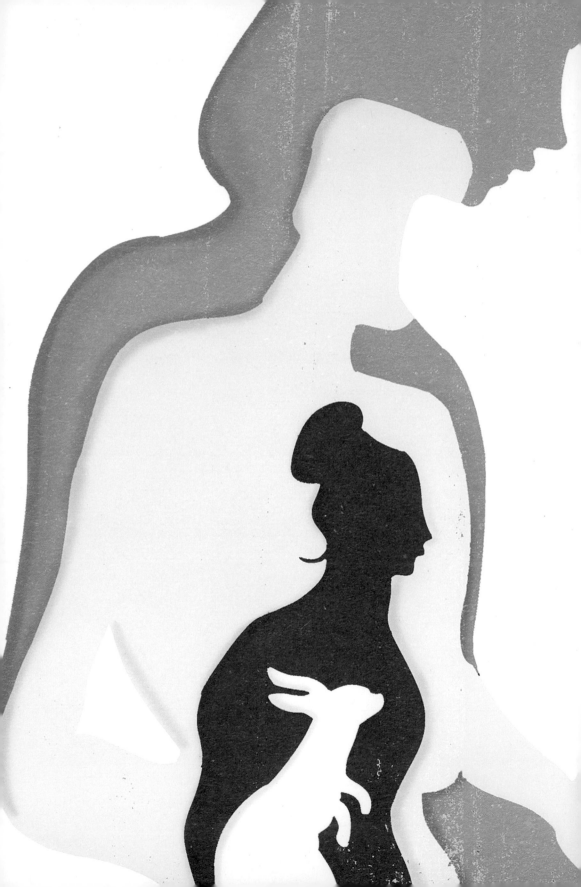

DREAMERS IN BROAD DAYLIGHT: TEN CONVERSATIONS

Leslie Jamison

ILLUSTRATION BY Eve Liu

I: DESIRE

ONCE UPON A TIME I met a stranger and in my mind we lived an entire life together. Not just one life, but many lives. Not just once, but many times.

This particular stranger was a lawyer in Portland. I'd come to his office because someone told me there was going to be a protest. There was no protest. I ended up sitting in a corporate conference room with this lawyer in his sage-green fleece vest. We talked about the pipeline that was getting laid near tribal lands in Standing Rock. Beneath his justifications, I could sense a white man's deep sorrow for the crimes of his country. That sorrow was the part of him I imagined building a life with.

My conversation with this lawyer lasted only an hour. But by the time I left, I'd already begun to spin an elaborate fantasy about how our single conversation might change his life. It would force a reckoning with his conscience. He'd remember why he went into law in the first place. He would look up my website! The next time he came to New York, we would have a tryst at a swank Midtown hotel. Maybe the one with the burger joint behind the red velvet curtain. He'd leave his marriage. (The internet told me he was married. But no matter! I was married, too.) The rapid current of my daydream flowed easily around our spouses like two boulders in a river. We would move into a Craftsman bungalow painted the same shade of sage green as his fleece vest. He would save the world by fighting environmental injustice. I would save the world by writing literary essays. We'd watch

prestige television once a week. On all the other nights, we wouldn't need TV; we'd have too much to talk about.

These daydreams occupied the better portion of my flight back east. Back home, they filled all the crevices of my domestic labors. They followed me for weeks, as I walked along the damp sidewalks of Brooklyn, past brownstones whose lit windows exposed perfect lives in which no one needed to dream about living anywhere else. Which was my ultimate daydream: imagining a life in which I no longer daydreamed at all.

I've spent my whole life daydreaming. It embarrasses me to think of tallying the hours. It feels like ingratitude. It feels like infidelity. It's often been *about* infidelity. I've daydreamed while walking, while running, while drinking, while smoking—sitting in the Boston cold, seventeen years old, daydreams sprouting like so many weeds from the cracked sidewalk of a broken heart. I've daydreamed on every form of transport—something about commuting feels conducive to daydreaming, the pockets of time in between our commitments, and the fact of the body in motion, neither here nor there, available for an elsewhere. I've daydreamed to music and in silence, in solitude and in company. It's hardly exceptional. Studies have found that daydreaming accounts for between a quarter and a half of our waking hours, that we do it every few minutes, during nearly every activity except sex. Eric Klinger, a psychologist at the University of Minnesota, claims that daydreams make up about half the average person's thoughts.

My first daydreams were crushes. In one fantasy, the blond baseball player from my physics class walked up to the front of the room and announced— against a backdrop of velocity and momentum equations—that he wanted to go to prom with me. "She might seem quiet," he would tell the class. "But once you get to know her, she really has so much to say." Sometimes I'd revise midstream: He wouldn't say, She really has so much to say. That was something my middle-aged mom would say. He'd say, She's pretty awesome.

In college, when I worked part-time as an assistant to an immigration lawyer, I daydreamed about making an important discovery that would help secure asylum for one of our clients. I would rush into the courtroom with neatly highlighted papers. The family would be saved. The courtroom would react with hushed voices: Who was that . . . ?

When I restricted my eating, my daydreams grew more restricted, too: they started to be almost entirely about food. I looked up restaurant menus and imagined eating all the dishes they listed: chocolate bread pudding with rum-caramelized bananas, or Ritz cracker–crusted scrod with herbed potatoes. My hunger was so bottomless it could be satisfied only in fantasies.

Near the end of my marriage, I spent more and more time in my fantasies. My daydreams were imagined affairs, or else counterfactuals in which I'd married someone else. As the psychoanalyst Adam Phillips argues, "Any ideal, any preferred world, is a way of asking, what kind of world are we living in that makes this the solution . . . What would the symptom have to be for this to be the self-cure?" My daydreams were the destruction, and the oxygen. They were a whispered diagnosis, a truth serum.

After we eventually separated, I looked back on my daydreams with a mixture of gratitude and shame. Had they been toxic evasions, a way of disappearing into fantasy to avoid the work of saving my marriage? Or were they necessary articulations of desire—something less like cowardice, and more like a summons?

II: SHAME

Over dinner with strangers in Rochester—on a work trip, a few months after my eventual separation—I brought up daydreaming because I was desperate to change the subject. The subject was our actual lives. My hosts were asking about my husband and our young daughter. I didn't want to tell them we were getting divorced. I was tired of saying, It's for the best, or, It's very painful, in a perfectly calibrated tone that suggested both sadness and composure.

My hosts were two professors who had been married for several decades. The woman was very talkative. Her husband was not. I started doing that thing where I projected unrealistic levels of domestic bliss onto this pair while simultaneously suspecting I wouldn't have been able to stand being married to either one of them.

At a certain point, I thought, Fuck it, and started asking them about their daydreams. The talkative woman was adamant: she didn't have daydreams. Did I? How could I possibly have enough time to daydream? She certainly didn't.

"I don't know," I said lamely. "I do it on the subway?"

At this point in my life, I was the single mother of a sixteen-month-old baby, with a full-time job as a professor and another full-time job as a writer and a third full-time job as a Person Getting Divorced, so I didn't necessarily have a lot of free time. But I found time for daydreaming anyway. I've never not found time for daydreaming.

The woman in Rochester nailed my shame precisely. Or rather, one of my shames: the shame of indolence, leisure, privilege, and waste.

She asked, "What do you daydream about?"

I had a perverse impulse to say the most embarrassing thing. I said sometimes I daydreamed about winning a Pulitzer. The talkative woman said, "There you go! I would never feel entitled to do that." Which made me feel ashamed in an entirely different way.

In the midst of our fervent back-and-forth, the woman's quiet husband said, very quietly, "I daydream all the time."

He spoke so softly I barely heard him. But his wife heard him. She asked him—as she'd asked me—what he daydreamed about. He said nothing. She said, "Go on, you can say. I don't mind." He fiddled with the handle of his coffee cup. "No really," she said. "You can say."

But he didn't say, and I was glad. I wanted him to keep his daydreams for himself. I wanted him to have something that was just his own.

My shame about daydreaming is the shame of solipsism and self-centered fantasy, the shame of turning from the banality of daily life toward the hollow calories of wish fulfillment, the shame of preferring the hypothetical to the actual.

In high school, the shame of my crushes was mainly a function of their asymmetry: wanting a boy so much more than he wanted me. But as I got older, the kernel of my shame migrated a few degrees to the left. It was less about my crushes as inherently asymmetrical (sometimes they were reciprocated), and more about my crushes as reductive: the fantasy relationship is entirely composed of revelation and crisis, all inflection point rather than stasis, none of the ordinary, uncinematic moments from which closeness is actually forged.

On Wild Minds, an online forum for people who struggle with excessive daydreaming, a thirty-year-old woman who had been having the same daydream about dating a rock star since her early teens put up a post titled "Killing your main character?" She wrote,

> Sometimes I feel like the daydream is trying to break through into the front of my mind so I took action and killed my character. She (me) died and my daydreaming stopped for a couple of weeks . . . Now I have a new 'me' in daydreams and . . . I've spent three days lying on my bed literally just daydreaming. I know if I just kill another character in my head another will show up.

My shame attaches to the persistence of my daydreams as much as their content. It rises from their whack-a-mole constancy: no matter what I have, I'll always fantasize about something else. My daydreaming habit tethers an impulse to its punishment: boundless freedom alongside the shame of wanting this freedom. I force myself to go hours without a fantasy, then finally indulge one, tip into its soft unmade bed; then force myself out of bed again, back to the work of the real.

Restraint. Indulgence. Punishment. This triptych of impulses has structured my relationship to desire for so long: with food, booze, men. The shame of fantasy has always felt related to my bottomless appetite for sweet things, for the dessert before the dessert, for dessert for breakfast, for desserts that contain *other* desserts: bowls of melted peanut butter ice cream with a peanut butter cookie batter swirl. The spun sugar of fantasy never leaves you satisfied. It leaves you feeling as if you ate too much, and also nothing at all. Which is the shame of the daydream: too much, and nothing at all.

III: SURVIVAL

A few weeks after my husband and I separated, my friend Emma came over to the dark railroad sublet I was renting with my daughter. It was the middle of winter. The apartment got very little light. Another friend called it our birth canal because it was long and narrow: a little bit claustrophobic, but also a threshold.

Emma was also at a threshold. After spending most of her adult life in New York, she was moving to Los Angeles. She told me she was having a lot of daydreams about what her life in California would be like. Even though she knew her daydreams wouldn't come true precisely as she imagined, they were a useful placeholder, more inviting than a blank space. These fantasies helped her believe in the possibility of another life. They granted it texture.

Between 1983 and 1985, the artist Jenny Holzer debuted her *Survival Series:* a set of slogans displayed on large electronic billboards in public spaces. My favorite, which has since graced postcards, condom wrappers, moving vans, and marble benches, is this one: IN A DREAM YOU SAW A WAY TO SURVIVE AND YOU WERE FULL OF JOY.

One of my deepest beliefs about life is that it will never play out exactly as we imagine. If that's true, then every daydream is a little death—a foreclosure of possibility rather than its conjuring. But Emma offered another way of seeing this: the daydream was never the destination; it was just a path to get there. The daydreams I'd had during the end of my marriage weren't prophecies. They just built a bridge off the edge of a cliff.

IV: DIFFERENCE

Over dinner one night—at the cusp of summer, six months into my separation— my friend Tara mused that perhaps people fall into two camps: they daydream about possible things, or impossible ones. We were at her apartment, sitting in her cluttered kitchen around a rough-hewn wooden table spread with bowls of lamb stew and saffron rice, hunks of beetroot bread and buffalo-milk cheese, a peach tart we'd all ravaged. It was a night of excess. Conversation without edges. My sobriety breathed the fumes of everyone else's white-wine buzz.

I'd been telling Tara about my own daydreams—how they'd almost always been about romance, and the shame I felt at that, as if it testified to a certain poverty of imagination. When I asked her what she daydreamed about, she pointed at the ceiling above our heads, where her neighbor lived with a rabbit who had been rescued a few weeks earlier. "I don't daydream about crushes. I daydream about the rabbit who lives upstairs," Tara said. "I imagine what it would be like to *be her.*"

Once I started asking other people about their daydreams, I began to realize that daydreams are like pain: impossible to compare across the bodies of dreamers. Different in texture, different in intensity, different in constancy: all the time might mean once an hour to one person, once a minute to another. No Greenwich Mean Time for our inner fantasy lives. One person might say "Google stalk" and mean glancing at a Wikipedia page, but to me it means getting to the bottom of the fourth page of search results, or the ninth, to the article someone's mother once published in a neighborhood newspaper recounting her childhood vacations to an island off the coast of Maine.

It started to seem like other people's daydreams were secrets they kept hidden in plain sight. They fantasized in front of me all the time—on the subway and the sidewalk, in my classes—but I had no idea what movies played inside their heads, or hummed at the tips of their tongues, perpetually unspoken. Some people understand daydreaming as a generative mode of self-actualization, à la The Secret—the world will give you what you visualize getting—while other people tuck it away like a form of chronic masturbation. On Reddit message boards, daydreamers have created massive crowdsourced catalogues of their daydreaming content: playing every instrument and singing vocals in favorite songs; taking out a high-school gunman; winning the lottery and starting a trash collection business to clean up outer space; lying upside-down and imagining what it would be like to walk on the ceiling of everything; taking revenge against the guy in traffic who cut them off without signaling.

Once I started asking people about their daydreams, it felt like the psychic equivalent of a coffee table book I loved as a child, featuring full of photos of people posed in front of their homes with all of their material possessions, rugs and chairs and pots and pans, stacked on the lawn, or the curb, or the icy field. People piled their daydreams in front of me like used razors and couch cushions and vibrators. One friend told me, "I used to daydream about men, now I daydream about the books I want to write." Another friend told me that her daydreams aren't like little films at all. She has trouble summoning visuals in her mind's eye, and her daydreams are mainly imagined dialogues. "Almost like a radio play," she said. Some people's daydreams aren't even narrative. They're more like poems. One friend told me that when she was a teenager full of suicidal thoughts, she would have a specific fantasy of her head filling up with Civil War bullets, the silver balls slowly darkening the round globe of her skull like a gumball machine.

In his seminal 1966 book, *Daydreaming: An Introduction to the Experimental Study of Inner Experience*, the Yale psychologist Jerome L. Singer argues that daydreaming can serve an adaptive purpose in people's lives, helping them attend more closely to their inner lives, manage their emotions, and solve frustrating problems. In the same year, he and John Antrobus (who had been his first doctoral student) released the Imaginal Processes Inventory, a questionnaire with 344 statements designed to gather information about the frequency and content of people's daydreams, as well as the role these daydreams played in their daily lives. Over his years of research, Singer outlined three broad styles of daydreaming: positive-constructive daydreaming (characterized by playful, wishful, "planful" thinking), guilty-dysphoric daydreaming (characterized by anxious, obsessive, often failure-related fantasies), and poor attentional control (characterized by an inability to fully inhabit either the internal daydream or the external situation). Many psychologists before and after Singer have considered daydreaming in negative terms (focused on the detrimental effects of "mind wandering"), but much of Singer's research focused on the positive dimensions—specifically, daydreaming's correlation with creativity, problem-solving, constructive planning, and interpersonal curiosity. The scope of the statements on the IPI itself suggests the range of what this single term, daydream, might mean across the minds of various dreamers: I imagine myself failing those I love. The sounds I hear in my daydreams are clear and distinct. I picture myself being accepted into an organization for successful individuals only. In my daydreams, I feel guilty for having escaped punishment. The "pictures in my mind" seem as clear as photographs.

For some people, daydreams might involve abstract ideas; for others, they're highly granular sensory fantasies: a lover's gravelly British accent, the chlorinated ripple of a plunge pool in the Maldives. It's nearly impossible for me to daydream in the abstract. I never fantasized about the *idea* of getting the Pulitzer. Instead, I fantasized about getting the phone call as I'm out with my infant daughter strapped to my chest, running late for work, realizing I forgot to pack the boiled zucchini she needs for lunch. It's a fantasy in which all the banality of being a mother is interrupted, for a moment, by an extraordinary moment of being witnessed as something else: an artist, a genius, whatever. It would have been impossible to summon that fantasy without the sensory texture: my baby's onesie and my own shirt dampened with sweat, the sweet almond of her shampoo, the rise of her curls beneath my chin, the crush of strollers on the morning sidewalks.

"Our lives become an elegy to needs unmet and desires sacrificed, to possibilities refused, to roads not taken," Phillips writes. "We can't imagine our lives without the unlived lives they contain."

But I don't agree with Phillips when he says that "the right choice is the one that makes us lose interest in the alternatives," and I suspect he doesn't even agree fully with himself. It's a delusion—a fantasy of certainty—to think there's a path that could make anyone stop wondering about the other paths. My friend Anna tells me, "I feel sure that depression is when you don't know what you daydream about." Daydreams aren't questions to be answered, but questions to live with, dangerous only when they stay static. Even in our best lives, our daydreams allow us to retain secret lives that no one else can access or touch. They are the ultimate privacy: the thing that remains secret even inside our closest intimacies, perhaps the thing that exists in order to remain private within those intimacies. The things we imagine doing are more private than any of the things we've done.

V: PLAY

On a late-summer afternoon, on a strip of grass beside the East River, my daughter was zipping herself into a ghost suit. She was three-and-a-half years old, and impossible to photograph; she was always in motion. On this day, she was creating an imaginary county fair using the grass, rocks, stairs, and bike-racks of the park: the ghost ride, the bear ride, the underworld ride, and the vacuum cleaner ride. Just a month earlier, we'd gone to an actual county fair upstate in New Paltz, taken a Ferris wheel high into a bruised purple sky. Like the actual rides we'd gone on, these invented rides imposed reliable commands—step in, zip up, buckle up, go here—onto situations that might otherwise be frightening. Step-by-step instructions for navigating overwhelm.

In his theory of daydreaming, Sigmund Freud links the imaginary play of childhood not only to adult daydreaming but also to an artist's work:

> Might we not say that every child at play behaves like a creative writer, in that he creates a world of his own, or rather, rearranges the things of this world in a new way which pleases him? It would be wrong to think he does not take that world seriously; on the contrary, he takes his play very seriously and he expends large amounts of emotion on it. The opposite of play is not what is serious but what is real.

A half-century later, the psychologist D. W. Winnicott also proposed a connection between childhood play and adult daydreaming—but while Freud is invested in the connections between childhood play and creative inspiration, Winnicott is most interested in daydreaming as an extension of childhood self-soothing practices. Winnicott's famous theory of the "good-enough mother" holds that while a mother initially adapts herself almost entirely to the needs of her child, over time her child is increasingly able to endure her "failures" to meet the child's needs completely. This capacity takes the form of physical self-soothing (thumb-sucking), transitional objects, and ultimately more sophisticated internal processes of "remembering, reliving, fantasying, dreaming." In this framework, daydreams start as an adaptive coping mechanism, but they can also become—in adulthood—a way of disassociating from the frustrations of reality rather than tolerating them.

Freud and Winnicott offer two different ways of understanding daydreaming: daydreaming as a manifestation of the artist in everyone—a type of casual, everyday creative production—or daydreaming as a crutch, an adult form of thumb-sucking, a way of ducking away from the stress, uncertainty, or overwhelm of daily life.

Perhaps these are not two categorically different ways of understanding daydreaming, but one way to start constructing a taxonomy of daydreams: richly generative fantasies versus the cul-de-sac of a coping mechanism. Do our daydreams build something, or simply run away from something else? And if they can do both, how do we become aware of which one they are doing? When does desire lead us somewhere useful, and when does it simply make it impossible for us to be wherever we are?

VI: CREATION

In December 1907, in the offices of a Vienna bookseller, Freud delivered a lecture called "Creative Writers and Daydreaming" to a small crowd of around ninety people. "May we really attempt to compare the imaginative writer with the 'dreamer in broad daylight' [*Der traumer am hellichten Tag*] and his creations with daydreams?" he asked. The answer was yes. Just as we can read romance novels and adventures with confidence, Freud argued, knowing that nothing will happen to the protagonist "under the protection of a special Providence," so a daydreamer operates with a kind of impunity, knowing he enjoys the "special Providence" of being the story's author as well as its central character. "Through this revealing characteristic of invulnerability," Freud observed, "we can immediately recognize His Majesty the Ego, the hero alike of every daydream and of every story."

Whenever I take up Freud's invitation to regard the creative writer as a professionalized daydreamer, I imagine Harold, the hero of *Harold and the Purple Crayon,* who draws the landscape he inhabits, full of hot-air balloons and picnics, using more fantasy to solve the problems that his fantasies create: When he draws too many pies for his picnic, he draws a moose and a porcupine to eat them up. When he tires of his fantasy, he draws his own bed to return to. There's a certain kind of daydreaming that involves not just manipulating the terms of the world but actually building them—or rebuilding them. During high school, I assumed my crushes were about the boys, but looking back, I can see they were always about the girls: my friends, my co-authors. The boys were just ciphers, a pretext for our elaborate collaborations.

In 1971, a group of female artists led by Judy Chicago and Miriam Schapiro created Womanhouse, which they called a "repository of daydreams." They converted an abandoned mansion in Hollywood into a collection of whimsical, fantastical, and polemical environments: Chicago's *Menstruation Bathroom* (a white bathroom filled with nothing but menstruation products, a trash can overflowing with bloody tampons, and a clothesline strung with bloody pads); Faith Wilding's *Womb Room* (a giant crocheted spiderweb); Sandy Orgel's *Linen Closet* (a female mannequin whose body had been sliced into pieces by the shelves that held her linens). As Chicago and Schapiro wrote in their catalogue essay, "The age-old female activity of homemaking was taken to fantasy proportions. Womanhouse became the repository of the daydreams women have as they wash, bake, cook, sew, clean and iron their lives away."

Daydreaming often has political stakes: intrinsically anti-capitalist because it doesn't "produce" anything—though its content is often deeply aspirational, structured by capitalism—it's also an activity that workers can do alongside the labor they've been forced to do, whether it's manual or domestic, clerical or janitorial; whether it involves caregiving or production.

On Wild Minds, a seventy-four-year-old retired graphic designer shares that she has been expanding the same "enormous soap opera" since childhood: "Since I was four years old I have invented secret, fictional characters in huge quantities and spent hours each day fine tuning and developing these 'people' . . . an elaborate inner world of over 200 characters." After the trauma of being sent away to boarding school at the age of eight, her daydreams grew more "pathological": "My fantasies are like watching a film, with I the creator but not in it as myself . . . The content became progressively detailed, their families, appearance, age with birth dates, height, interests . . . I also indulged in mantras of their private, special names."

Even the language she uses to describe her daydreams begins to map her conflicted feelings: "pathological" but also sustaining, how she "indulged" in the reciting of their "private, special names." She has always been at the core—the godly director—but never part of the show; her entire life has played out alongside this shadow world. "Owing to its intense gratification, I have never been able to let it go."

In Freud's description of the "revealing characteristic of invulnerability" at the core of every daydream, I see one explanation for why daydreams often include so much darkness, peril, and trouble: Invulnerability is made most visible by trouble. It's only by getting close to danger and evading it that we can feel ourselves impervious to it.

One user on Wild Minds started an entire thread about negative daydreams, on which people shared how they invented traumatic situations in order to imagine themselves rescuing someone or being rescued, or even more banal examples: daydreaming bossy people and then imagining how they could be encouraged to change.

In one recurring fantasy that I had near the end of my marriage, I was married to a war correspondent, and while I was pregnant with his child he got abducted by ISIS and held hostage for months. There was a reel of film I played again and again: My body crossing the tarmac toward his army plane, with the wind lifting my hair as I watched his emaciated body descending the steps, kneeling in front of me, kissing my belly. Sometimes the fantasy was in first person, and I was seeing everything through my own eyes; other times it was in third person, and I watched us from above.

It's shameful to confess a daydream like this—though I suspect many people have them—because it feels like exploitation, as if I plucked some abstracted, operatic pain from a Hollywood premise, connected to the actual suffering of others, and called it my own in an attempt to brush up against a powerful feeling.

Shameful as it was, there was still a reason I was doing it. "You can't treat your anorexia as something that's merely destroying you," a therapist once told me. "You have to ask what it's giving you. What you get from it."

Constructing this hypothetical version of myself, facing the abduction of my war-correspondent husband, offered relief from the far more mundane pain that saturated my days: googling "divorced while pregnant" to see if others had done it. My real-life pain was ordinary and unresolved. It had no structure of crisis and relief. In the fantasy of capture and return, the reunion on the tarmac, the roar of engines drowning our voices, I found the consoling purity of unequivocal feeling states: fear and love. It was a fantasy of emotional simplicity: melodrama as antidote to the muddled emotional contradictions of reality. In a life-and-death scenario, romantic ambivalence is beside the point. The point is staying alive. The point is being together again. The harder parts of being together again—boredom, claustrophobia, the sour whiff of vulnerability—have no footing in the stark chiaroscuro of peril and salvation.

In the bold plotlines of dark daydreams, the danger is entirely external. A relationship isn't threatened by the internal demons of anger, resentment, distance. It's threatened by terrorists! The call is no longer coming from inside the house. But that's the inevitable betrayal of daydreaming: even when you outsource the trouble, the call is always coming from inside the house.

VII: NET

After my separation, I'd often scroll through Zillow to find the blueprints of other lives: a cedar house near Anchorage with a dodecagon living room, or a white farmhouse in Maine with hydrangeas crowding the gravel driveway and the perfect blue-raspberry lozenge of a swimming pool in back. In all these houses, I always found myself looking for windows—as if I suspected I would always daydream about somewhere else, like the boy who used his last wish from the genie to wish for a thousand more.

The internet has changed the terms of our daydreaming. On Zillow, a thousand different houses offer a thousand different versions of yourself. Other people's Instagram accounts build our daydreams for us. TikTok externalizes our fantasies. The internet grants our daydreams fodder, but it also takes away their breathing room. It fills in too many gaps. It's harder to imagine a Cape Cod wedding with the guy from your college newspaper when your Facebook feed holds a thousand photos of him holding his newborn son. The internet dissolves the buffer between having a crush on someone and stalking him. It makes you feel like you've already driven past his house six times that night.

When I asked Padya, my twenty-six-year old research assistant, about their daydreams, they told me about being a teenager in Bangladesh—getting deeply immersed in Tumblr, where people discussed the plotlines of their favorite television shows. Padya started to imagine the discussions that strangers would have about Padya's life, if it were a television show: which characters people would love, which ones they'd hate; which narrative twists they'd adore, which ones they'd despise. More than Padya imagined the television show of their life, they imagined the comments *about* the show of their life. Imagining one's life as a television show felt familiar, but imagining this meta-level discourse *about* the show felt more specifically born of the digital era—in which reactions *are* the show, as much as the show itself.

Instagram is like a buffet of daydreams: all you can eat, and none of it yours. A beautiful woman sails the world on a catamaran with her sun-kissed sons. A surfer posts dream-filtered beach sunsets, tube riding, and breakfast smoothies. At @dumpedwifesrevenge, an Australian divorcée posts photographs of herself living her best life—wearing animal-print spandex, holding the setting sun perched on her fingertips—but also situates this daydream in relation to her "bumps." Her Instagram bio reads: "Dumped for the younger woman after 26 years. My revenge-BE FABULOUS & LOOK FABULOUS." She sees her Instagram feed as a response to the "challenge" of what her ex told her when their marriage was ending: "When two people have been together for a long time and they break up, there's always one who thrives and one who doesn't." For the Dumped Wife, cultivating her own life as daydream—professionally photographed—is an act of rebellion and survival.

The rabbit holes of the internet literalize the rhythms of associational thinking, turning mind-wandering into something full of clicks and visuals: You scan the Instagram account of Dumped Wife's Revenge; you google her name; you find an article about her life, and read that her beach town in southwestern Australia is a "holiday haven for Australia's elite"; you google "most expensive hotel in Eagle Bay"; you imagine yourself staying at a four-bedroom beach villa with an unbroken view of the turquoise Indian Ocean; you google "trees of southwestern Australia" to figure out what tree is in the corner of the shot—eucalyptus! or maybe banksia—and you google the dumped wife + "younger boyfriend." You imagine yourself in the hotel. You imagine yourself in her house. You imagine yourself writing an article about her life. You imagine yourself fucking a younger boyfriend whose face you haven't seen, whose existence you haven't confirmed. You pivot from speculation (imagining her life) to projection (imagining yourself in her life) and back again. These are the zigzags of a daydreaming mind, but now you can find images to give them life. The abstract daydream becomes six tabs spread across the top of your browser, like a trail of bread crumbs leading the way back into your maze of desire. You, your, yours. The second person like a smoke signal of shame. My browser, my desires.

Perhaps no social media embodies our daydreams more fully than TikTok, on which people act out their daydreams, make fun of themselves daydreaming, reproduce the interiors of their daydreams as absurd picaresque microdramas: endless food without calories, fantasies of flight. The TikTok phenomenon that most accurately externalizes it all, however, is the POV video—a clip that invites the viewer to inhabit a particular scenario, often saturated with the excruciating emotional stakes of being a teenager. Some feel like exposure therapy: a sweet girl in a yellow floral smocked blouse invites you to imagine "ur teacher lets u pick partners but u have 2 friends in ur class who partnered up," or "there's not enough seats at the lunch table today, so you have no where to sit." It's almost like Edmund Burke's idea of the sublime: encountering danger from a position of safety.

Other POV videos look more like wish fulfillment: In one TikTok that's been hearted more than two million times, a bespectacled, sweet-faced boy with a baggy striped shirt says, "#pov you dont have a lunch at school and i offer you my entire lunch because I want you to be okay." @idrinkvapejuice has gotten more than six hundred thousand hearts on a TikTok captioned, "POV: i'm ur dumb jock crush. you tell me you're feeling depressed. i try to make it better." The girl mimes someone who has little experience with sadness, but real compassion for it—or at least, real compassion for a girl with a nice ass:

"Depressed?" she says slowly. "Don't. Be. Sad. You are so thick."

Watching this TikTok, even just reading its caption, is like reading the CliffsNotes version of my deepest desires, outsourced to the internet. How many times have I played through some version of this fantasy: That my sadness could make me desirable? That it could solicit someone's love, or at least his attention? One siren call of social media is that we might see our desires given shape before we even have to shape them ourselves, that someone else might do the work of wanting for us, that we could outsource this labor, as we have outsourced so many others.

VIII: ESCAPE

Over dinner, my friend Adrian told me about the recurring daydream he used to have during his time at reform school. This was a boarding school he'd been taken to against his will, as a teenager, in a nightmarish scenario in which strangers came into his bedroom in the middle of the night and took him to a car waiting outside. It was a removal designed to make him feel as if he had no control over his body. So it didn't surprise me that his daydream was about bodily escape.

During their mandatory group therapy sessions, he would gaze at a massive window—directly across from his assigned seat—and imagine running straight through it. It was a fantasy of sudden rupture as relief in the midst of ongoing tedium. He wouldn't imagine this abstractly, but in a very detailed, almost pragmatic way: what angle he should run from, how he should position his body so it wouldn't be injured by the broken glass. He imagined the feeling of the glass shattering around his moving body—the pressure and release, the sharpness, the crackling of shards.

It might seem counterintuitive to get tangled in the pragmatics of a daydream, given that part of the point of a daydream is its ability to transcend the pragmatic. In a fantasy, my friend could have made himself immune to broken glass. I could have made the Portland lawyer unmarried. But that somehow feels like cheating. A frictionless daydream feels like vapor. There's more traction when you let reality poke through the dream—like splinters emerging from the grain of the wood, catching in the palm.

"It's funny how we still want the laws of gravity to apply in our daydreams," I told my friend. "We don't want them to happen on the moon."

"We want real life to happen on the moon," he agreed. "We want our daydreams to happen here on Earth."

IX: COMPULSION

One evening at dusk, a patient sat with her psychotherapist, none other than Donald Winnicott, and confessed that even while they were talking about her daydreaming compulsion, she was daydreaming. Pointing at the sliver of sky she could see through his office window, she told him, "I am up on those pink clouds where I can walk," and then asked if he thought her fantasy was generative or toxic: "When I am walking up on that pink cloud, is that my imagination enriching life or is it this thing that you are calling fantasying which happens when I am doing nothing and which makes me feel that I do not exist?" Over the course of their sessions together, Winnicott had been distinguishing between imagination—a kind of speculation connected to real life, like looking forward to a holiday—and "fantasying," a more dissociative state in which some nominal physical activity—smoking compulsively, or playing solitaire for hours—becomes a cover for compulsive daydreaming. "In the fantasying," he writes, "what happens happens immediately, except that it does not happen at all." Over the course of decades devoted to these fantasies, he wrote, his patient "managed to construct a life in which nothing that was really happening was fully significant to her."

The phrase "maladaptive daydreaming" was first coined in 2002 by Dr. Eli Somer, a professor of clinical psychology at the University of Haifa, who defined it as "extensive fantasy activity that replaces human interaction and/or interferes with academic, interpersonal, or vocational functioning." In 2017, Somer founded the International Consortium for Maladaptive Daydreaming Research, and developed a sixteen-point scale called the MDS-16, which includes questions such as, "When the real world interrupts one of your daydreams, how annoyed do you feel?"

In a 2011 survey of ninety "self-identified non-normative fantasizers," researchers Jayne Bigelsen and Cynthia Schupak found patterns of intoxication and deflation reminiscent of other addictions. "Going into a daydream is very exciting," one participant said. "The feeling is almost like a kind of euphoria . . . As time passes, I quickly begin to feel locked in, like I can't let go. Reality always seems harder to face when I'm in a daydream or trying to come out of one." Another one wrote, "The amount of time you feel you have wasted with an imaginary community whilst neglecting your loved ones in reality brings about an enormous sense of guilt." A third said simply, "I just want to function a normal day without being someone else in my mind, without having to play this story."

X: DEATH

In a bakery by the East River, around the corner from my daughter's preschool, I asked my mom about her daydreams. I don't know exactly what I was expecting, except that I've often constructed my mother as an idealized mirror image of myself: adjacent, but superior. We're both emotionally perceptive, but she's more selfless. We were both working moms, but I work on literary essays and she worked on maternal health in the developing world. While I devoted my twenties to the full-time work of emotional volatility, she was devoting her sixties to getting arrested in her clerical collar at union strikes downtown. She fed me fresh-baked bread during my whole childhood; I feed my daughter a lot of take-out Thai.

She said it was harder now to have the kind of "building block" daydreams she used to have frequently: imagining the future that would be created by something she was doing in the present—speculating about what her kids would be like as adults, or her students' future careers. Now that she was seventy-seven, her life wasn't oriented toward the future in the same way. Now? my mom said. She sometimes fantasized about sharing a home with my aunt—her younger sister and best friend for seventy-three years—and she felt that even if this never came to pass, the daydream offered her a bridge: a way to think about the end of her life as something that would not be lonely or institutional.

Maybe youth is the native habitat of daydreams: the more possible futures in front of you, the more soil in which daydreams can take root. As we get older, our daydreams assume the shape of nostalgia or counterfactuals.

"These days," my mom continued, "some of my daydreams are about death." She didn't mean she wanted to die, just that she sometimes imagined what death might be like. This kind of daydreaming reminded her of being a child, fiercely determined to figure out how the world came to exist, unsatisfied with her father's answers. Eventually, she told him, "If you just tell me how it all got started, I can figure out the rest."

While we often long for narrative resolution, when the story is us, that kind of closure means psychic or literal death. Daydreams fight this closure by prolonging the narrative. They keep it unresolved. Imagining a life in which I don't daydream means imagining the death of a part of myself that I hate—but it's also a part of me that keeps me alive. A pulse of wondering. The nerve endings of alternatives. If daydreams are constantly forestalling the end of the story—constantly insisting, This life is not done—then how do you daydream the end of the story?

In her daydreams about death, my mother told me, she was often trying to imagine ways it might have some continuity with the life she's known so far— even as she knows that death is an experience defined by rupture. So much of daydreaming is about escape and alternatives—about imagining difference, envisioning an outside to your life—but this kind of daydreaming, the kind my mother described, is about the opposite. It's about imagining how things might stay the same. It's about imagining how some parts of ourselves might follow, even as we leave the world—or how a version of us might already be out there, somehow waiting. ⨍

ART PORTFOLIO: KUDZANAI-VIOLET HWAMI

Text by TIANA REID

Eve on Psilocybin, 2018
Oil on canvas, 51 ⅛ x 54 ⅜".
© Kudzanai-Violet Hwami.
Courtesy the artist
and Victoria Miro.

OPPOSITE

Bira, 2019
Oil on canvas, 71 x 59".
Commissioned by Gasworks.
Courtesy the artist
and Tyburn Gallery.
Photo: Andy Keate.

A QUIET, SOMETIMES imperceptible bliss drips over Kudzanai-Violet Hwami's paintings. In *Eve on Psilocybin* (2018), Eve is naked, grinning, and high on shrooms, but the artist's representations of other highs are subtler. In *You are killing my spirit* (2021), the subject lies back on a bed, eyes closed, one arm almost reaching to the viewer, the other floating limply in the air. The legs are in a constructive rest—knees bent, falling into each other, feet flat on the bedding, hip width apart. Behind everything is a picture within a picture, encased by a pink trim: a number of obscured faces that seem to be gazing at the reposing figure with a certain madness. The faces

You are killing my spirit, 2021
Oil on canvas, 60 ¼ x 102 ⅛".
© Kudzanai-Violet Hwami.
Courtesy the artist and Victoria Miro.

are a limbo-like audience, half there, half not there, waiting and anticipating. But somehow these portraits avoid the feeling that these figures (who are Hwami's family and friends or the artist herself) are being looked at. Through Hwami's eye, the exchange is tender and unafraid.

In the nudes *Expiation* (2021) and *Dance of Many Hands* (2017), Hwami manages a sexuality that is relaxed yet aware. It's a sexuality that almost seems to lean back. In *Mwana wa Mukami* (2016), a person sits back comfortably against a reading chair with shelves of books in the background. The subject's body is sketched out in gray, but most of the books are imaginatively colored: mulberry, marigold, forest green, turquoise, tangerine.

Little yellow devilish horns, adorned with squiggly marks, protrude from a partially furrowed brow. Hwami is interested in introspection, but her work still exudes a jagged-edged playfulness.

Hwami was born in Gutu, Zimbabwe, in 1993. She lived in South Africa until the age of seventeen, then moved to the UK, where she now lives and works.

Dance of Many Hands, 2017
Oil and acrylic on canvas,
86 ⅝ x 67". © Kudzanai-Violet Hwami.
Courtesy the artist and Victoria Miro.

OPPOSITE

Expiation, 2021
Oil, acrylic, oil stick, and silk screen on canvas,
50 ¼ x 47 ⅛". © Kudzanai-Violet Hwami.
Courtesy the artist and Victoria Miro.

Mwana wa Mukami, 2016
Pastel, charcoal, graphite,
pencil, and pen on paper.
59 x 59" Courtesy the artist
and Tyburn Gallery.

She has said of her trajectory, "With the collapsing of geography and time and space, no longer am I confined in a singular society but simultaneously I am experiencing Zimbabwe and South Africa and the UK, in my mind. I'm in the UK, but I carry those places with me everywhere I go." This collapse is apparent in her aptitude for collage. She incorporates old family photographs, vintage porn, and archival images from the internet. The effect is counterintuitive, one of both stripping and layering. Photographs are typically used to cement truth and fact, but Hwami unwinds all that, celebrating the idea of subjectivity.

With Hwami's artwork, interior life is a full-body high. The self grows crusty without the eye, trained to sense memories, shifts, analysis, feeling. Her paintings are evidence of small moments, big interventions. If you google Hwami, a bio will likely mention that she presented work at the Fifty-Eighth Venice Biennale in 2019 as part of the Zimbabwe Pavilion; she was the youngest artist ever to participate in the exhibition. But to claw at youth is a rigged game. Many of Hwami's subjects—Black, African, queer, young enough—are prone to being seen, if they are seen at all, as simple, infantilized. Hwami, however, sees them as they are, and as they might see themselves. ✦

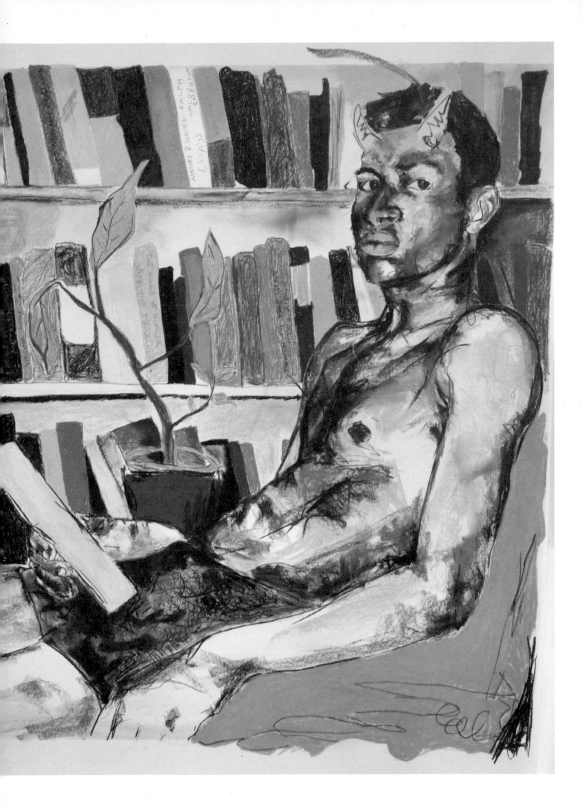

LOVE
Margaret Ross

I always try to memorize his face
but I never can. I can say
he has a face, he has
a body, an apartment.

He has a bowl of ice water
where he soaks his hands
because of tendons in his fingers.

He has a plant with long leaves
on the ledge above his toilet.

Once when I was there
and he had left the room
I wrote on a scrap of paper in my wallet
he's just a person
so I could read it
later, when I was home.

✦

I wait where a dirt path through a meadow
lets out at a gravel patch beside the paved road.
The air smells heavy, opulent.
Before the place the redwoods start
are orchards. The story is
my car broke down and he's
a stranger driving by.

Or I park on his street
and stand a minute gathering myself
behind the car. When I step out front, I'll see him
blue-lit, sitting by the window typing.
He won't hear me move until
I tap my knuckles to the glass.

It's hard to look at him right away
so I look at the white stretch
of his t-shirt.

The nubby lattice
pattern of the rug.

I step off my heels.
He wants me to kneel in front
of a mirror and say my name
and point to every part
of me that's his.

✦

At a party, a stranger
wearing nothing but a fishing net
embraces me because he loves
my friend, who wears a matching net
with shiny lures taped to her nipples.
A person in a Pilgrim costume
tells me how the person on the sofa
saved her marriage by becoming
what she calls their third. She met
the person in the park, their daughters
had the same name.

✦

When I ask him not to say my name
he thinks I'm saying names would feel
too close. They feel too distant.

He hands me the folded remnant
of a shirt he tore off me the week before.
I think you leave things here on purpose.
I didn't leave that, it's garbage.
You also left your hair thing.

Later, we watch a video of him
climb a cliff next to the ocean.
The day is cloudy, shadowless.
We watch his fingers feel out
angles on the rock and pull
his body higher.

Three thousand people
watched it before me.

From his bed
you see the dense crown
of a fig tree in the yard next door
where the tenant hung himself
last spring. Now blue tarp
curtains the house,
the landlord is renovating.

I feel a happiness so concentrated
it feels like fear.

✦

He has a lamp he softens
when I come, draping his shirt
over the shade.

He has a winding blue-green
helix tattooed up his side.

On my way, I stop
at gas stations and stand in the bathroom
checking. If you say the feeling out loud
it sounds comic, disproportionate.
I press brown paper towel
to my forehead.

ᚨ

Sun covered the bed.
I lay listening to him moving
through the other room, hearing
water, hearing something
open, shut, then silence
then him coming nearer.

How do you get close to a person?
Once you got past pleasure
there was pain. No
there was pleasure turning
into something pain was
part of. If you can let them
hurt you deep enough, you'll be
inside the other person.

Driving up nights on the freeway, dark fields
tearing by on either side, I practice
saying *hi. Hi.*

QUEEN, SLAVE, WOMAN

Fernanda Melchor

Translated from the SPANISH
by SOPHIE HUGHES

ILLUSTRATION BY Lorenzo Mattotti

"DOWNTOWN VERACRUZ IS FULL of ghosts," my father used to say whenever we went past his family's first home in the city, where they moved from Baja California: a gloomy tenement with a central courtyard on Avenida 5 de Mayo, now completely deserted. Like so many other buildings in the city's historic center, the shared house where my father took his first steps is today a rubble-filled ruin, a haunt for dipsomaniacs, mangy cats, and specters who languish among the rubbish and overgrown weeds and, every so often, spook the fine people of Veracruz, as the legendary Headless Priest used to do, or the souls of the women raped and murdered by the Dutch pirate Laurens de Graaf's men in the colonial period. Ghosts in rags, sleeping off their hangovers on the ground in alleyways; ghouls in human form poking their drunken faces through the broken trellises on the balconies; silhouettes that, out of charity or sheer cunning, occupy the wreckages of those vast coral stone houses, old mansions that collapse onto the pavement below, on windy days sometimes fatally, to the total indifference of their lawful owners, criollo big shots who would rather sit back and watch their inheritance fall to pieces than use up time, money, and influence on restoring this heritage site.

The National Lottery building on Independencia, while nowhere near as old as many of the derelict houses steadily crumbling into the downtown streets, forms part of this ghostly panorama: a labyrinth of apartments, offices, and shops distributed across six floors and still occupied by a handful of senior citizens who can't be evicted because of old tenancy laws—men and women who live by candlelight, without running water or electricity, and who tell stories of strange noises in the building's hallways: marbles and balls bouncing across the floors of boarded-up rooms, shouts and moans from those who perished in the fire that ravaged the building in the late seventies, or children's laughter and the patter of small feet going up and down the stairs.

Miguel, pensioner: "I lived in the National Lottery building for a long time, above Telas de México, the textiles shop on the corner of Calle Rayón and Independencia . . . It used to house the lottery offices, hence the name, but they moved when the fire broke out in Telas de México . . . After that, the building's owners came out with some crap about how they planned to renovate the apartments, but instead they cut off the electricity and water and ran us all out . . . I resisted because quite honestly, I couldn't afford to go anywhere else; I needed a rent-controlled apartment and that's why I clung on, but in the end the constant battle wore me down . . . And the truth is I never much liked living in that building . . . I don't know if you noticed when you went but it's got a bad vibe, don't you think? . . . Sort of like you can't relax in there, I can't explain it . . . And at night you hear horrible noises, screaming and groaning . . . We had a neighbor, Doña Esa, she's dead now but she was very sensitive to these things . . . She was the one who actually saw the two boys, Evangelina's sons, playing on the stairs, months after the crime was uncovered . . . I think that's why the owners let the place fall apart; maybe they just didn't want anyone to remember what had happened in that apartment."

On April 7, 1989, a story broke concerning apartment 501 of the National Lottery building: in a terrible fit of rage, a twenty-four-year-old woman had murdered her two young sons.

That incident alone would have provided enough material for weeks' worth of café gossip, before passing into merciful oblivion. But two specific details of the crime ensured that the story would transcend the tabloid crime pages to be written into popular legend: first, less than six years earlier, the offender, Evangelina Tejera Bosada, had been crowned the Queen of Veracruz Carnival, an honor that, even today, is widely considered the highest aspiration for any girl from an upstanding family in the city; and second, having repeatedly smashed her sons' skulls against the floor, Tejera Bosada went on to carve up their bodies and bury them in a large plant pot, which she then put out on her apartment balcony.

The first reports of Tejera Bosada's arrest and the discovery of the bodies of Jaime and Juan Miguel—ages three and two, respectively—appeared on Friday, April 7, 1989, in Veracruz's biggest newspapers. According to popular legend, however, the story began in the middle of March, when the residents of the National Lottery building supposedly detected a nasty smell. Only nineteen-year-old Juan Miguel Tejera Bosada, visiting his sister's apartment, dared to link the smell to the unexplained absence of his two little nephews.

In initial news reports, the young woman, described as pale and doleful, denied responsibility for the children's deaths. "I didn't kill my children," she declared before the court. "I just buried them after they died. My mother cut me off so I had no way of feeding them." Dressed in a men's T-shirt and dirty trainers, Tejera Bosada explained to Judge Carlos Rodríguez Moreno that her mother had stopped all financial support upon discovering that her daughter was pregnant and that the baby's father was married and had another family. The younger child, she confirmed, was fathered by the same man, Mario de la Rosa Villanueva, but since he had refused to legally acknowledge either of the two boys, Evangelina had registered them under her maiden name. She hadn't killed them, she vehemently maintained. The poor things had starved to death and she had merely tried to dispose of the bodies: first, on a makeshift paper pyre in her living room, and then, when that tactic failed, by cutting off their legs with a kitchen knife to make them fit inside a big Oaxacan pot, given to her by her mother months earlier.

José, journalist: "The court was packed with officials, reporters, and some sickos who came along just to hear the murderer's confession . . . She appeared behind bars; she looked like shit, the poor thing, hunched over and all scruffy in a skirt, trainers, and a white T-shirt that was way too big for her. Her blond hair was greasy and her chin was down by her chest . . . She never looked up the whole time she gave evidence, not once could I get a look at her eyes. It was like she was scared of people; she was holding on to the rusty bars and her hands were trembling . . . Her lawyer, Pedro García Reyes—Pistol Pete, we called him, because he was a thug like the Disney character—was perched on one of the female court clerks' desks, smoking furiously; he spent the whole hearing yelling at the prosecutor, Nohemí Quirasco, interrupting her cross-examination . . . When the time came, Evangelina said she hadn't killed her children, she claimed they'd starved to death because she couldn't afford to feed them, and she didn't mention anything to her family because they weren't on speaking terms . . . Then the prosecutor asked her why she'd buried the bodies in a pot and, damn, Evangelina just started shaking and said, "I was scared" . . . "Scared of what, or whom?" Quirasco asked, but that supercilious, overbearing prick Pedro objected to the question, on the grounds that it was irrelevant . . . To tell the truth, by this point I thought there was something fishy going on, like they were hiding something . . . That's why when the judge ordered all those psychiatric tests to be done right away, I predicted they were going to try to pass her off as mad, and look what happened . . ."

From her very first appearance before the judge, the reporters were openly skeptical of Tejera Bosada's statements, and went public with the medical examiner Gil Trujillo's conclusions: namely, that Jaime's and Juan Miguel's deaths had been caused by a series of closed head injuries and the two boys died several days apart, Juan Miguel first. In his April 7 article, Edgar Urrutia Hernández, a crime reporter for *El Dictamen*, claimed that Evangelina was a "compulsive liar," with a reputation for "regularly making up stories and living in fantasy land," while Héctor Ramón López, a correspondent for the *Diario de Xalapa*, described the event as "the most abhorrent case in the city's history," and repeatedly reminded his readers of Evangelina's profile as the "ex-carnival party queen who has turned into a schizophrenic woman charged with the horrific murder of her two children." Although the defendant claimed, in her first appearance before the judge, that she had previously undergone treatment with the psychiatrist Camerino Vázquez, the director of a small mental health clinic in the city, the public, whose moral outrage was supposedly reflected in the tabloid reports, would dismiss this as a lie, a "legal trick" to help Evangelina "circumvent criminal proceedings and evade punishment for her spine-chilling crime." Reporter Urrutia Hernández would also point out, in a story dated April 8, that the prosecution employed "a soft touch" when examining the defendant. The behavior of Judge Carlos Rodríguez Moreno was equally "paternalistic" when he voiced his suspicion that Tejera Bosada suffered from mental disorders, establishing a precedent that the accused and her defense would exploit to "bend the case in her favor," given the total absence of "proper legal rigor."

A group of lawyers from Veracruz, headed up by the ex-mayor Jorge Reyes Peralta, was convinced that the public would not settle for anything less than the harshest of punishments.

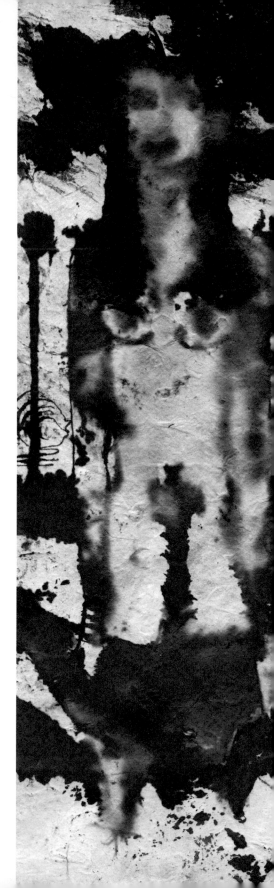

The team went to the Public Prosecutor's office the Monday after Tejera Bosada's detention and requested legal authorization to assist the prosecution and thus lawfully intervene in the trial against Tejera Bosada and prevent the defendant from evading justice by "feigning madness." In a statement to the press, Reyes Peralta—today the senior partner in one of the most powerful law firms in the city of Veracruz—stated that he was convinced beyond all doubt that Tejera Bosada had acted "with unprecedented cruelty in murdering her two young boys, for the sole purpose of causing nonmaterial damage to the father of those children—children she frequently and ruthlessly abused."

Neither the rumors that Evangelina Tejera had suffered from long-term mental illnesses— with symptoms including depression and uncontrollable violent outbursts—nor her thorny romantic relationship with Mario de la Rosa, nor her suspected use of illegal drugs mitigated her crime in any way. On the contrary: they were seen as aggravating factors, proof of the cynicism with which the wicked woman tried to evade justice in order to return to her life of ruin and vice.

But who was Evangelina Tejera Bosada? Who was this woman who, just six years earlier, had been crowned by the people of Veracruz as their glitzy queen, and was now being accused by the very same community of an unspeakable crime? How could this fair-haired beauty, only recently awarded the highest honor to which an unmarried Veracruz girl could aspire, have turned into the impassive waif now splashed all over the tabloid crime pages?

Tomasa, shopkeeper: "Oh yes, she was pretty, she could have almost passed for a gringa with her green eyes and pale skin . . . She'd started young with the boys; there was even one who knocked her about, but then she was a bit nuts herself, you know? . . .

167

She'd been a stoner since she was fifteen, but she really showed her true colors after she was crowned Carnival Queen, what with all the parties and hanging around in trendy clubs with the rich set . . . They say she only ever went with 'juniors,' daddy's boys who would snort a load of coke and then drive around in their fancy cars doing all sorts of crazy things; some of them even killed people, but nothing ever happened to them because the police were there only to cover for them . . . I remember that Picho Malpica, he killed Polo Hoyos's daughter just because the girl refused to go out with him; and there was Miguel Kayser, who dealt coke at all the parties . . . Some say he dealt to Evangelina and the boys' father, De la Rosa, and that they'd use the National Lottery building apartment to sell coke and marijuana to other addicts and have orgies . . . and that in one of those orgies she just flipped and killed the two kiddies . . ."

Born in 1965 to a stay-at-home mother—whose name didn't appear in any of the documents I consulted—and Jaime Tejera Suárez, an estate agent, Tejera Bosada was brought up in a home where, rumor has it, verbal and physical violence were the norm, at least until her parents' marriage fell apart. Under pressure from both her mother and the worsening economic crisis of the early eighties, a teenage Evangelina was forced to abandon her studies before completing secondary school, taking a job as a secretary for an import-export company in town. Tejera Bosada and her father grew closer after her mother remarried: he encouraged Evangelina to run for Carnival Queen in 1983, and according to the social pages published in February of that same year, he was the sole parent to attend, "with great emotion, the coronation of his beautiful daughter."

In Veracruz, the selection of the Carnival Queen has more to do with the candidate's socioeconomic status than with her physical attributes. The queen is chosen from a group of candidates according to her purchasing power—the crown is awarded to the woman with the highest number of votes, which are bought from the festival's organizing committee with hard cash. In the context of Mexico's 1982 debt crisis, Tejera Bosada's ascent to the Carnival throne necessarily suggests that her family (or at least her father) had the support of an entire network of contacts who were prepared to pay for votes as well as her royal trousseau. The social pages from the time entirely overlook such crude details, choosing instead to exalt Evangelina's grace and charm ("Her Majesty is eighteen years of age, enjoys playing tennis and piano, and is a great fan of contemporary music," read one profile in *El Dictamen*), as well as the way this "fair beauty" cheerfully represented "the joy of the Veracruz people," in "a reign of fantasy and illusion." The media played down both the violence that invariably took place on the city's streets during Carnival (the assaults, the sexual harassment and abuse, the public intoxication and often lethal injuries) and the grim sight of a Veracruz completely overrun by mobs of people, whom local writer Ignacio García, in an article from the time, compared to "Melquíades's raggedy band of gypsies arriving in a muddy Macondo." Instead, society reporters admired "the beautiful decorations and colorful lights," "the collective joy" of the Veracruz people, characterized by "their stupendous good humor and ability to see the bright side, their refusal to get worked up about the crisis or the fall in oil prices, or anything that might cast a shadow over their lives." In the words of reporter Alfonso Valencia Ríos, a representative of the city's pro-government media, Carnival let people "forget about the economic crisis eroding the country, forget about the lack of foreign exchange and the brutal inflation pulverizing salaries," offering instead "the pleasure of a marvelous parade of floats, troupes, and costumes," which were all examples of "the grace, beauty, inventiveness, wit, and creativity" of the Veracruz people.

It is here, at the height of this delirious party, this bacchanal of revelers doing its best to camouflage reality with confetti, tinsel, and booze, that the Veracruz myth locates the beginning of Evangelina Tejera Bosada's fall from grace. Moving from dance to dance, cavorting with the rich and powerful, Evangelina celebrates, drinks, smokes, and, most likely, takes drugs to keep up with the party, the one that only gets going after the official parade is over, when her formal gown, which looks like something out of nineteenth-century Austria-Hungary, is switched out for a fashionable top and jeans. In her escapades at Veracruz's late-night hot spots, during the endless processions along the city's coastline and at the social events where she's obliged to dance with anyone who asks, Evangelina dazzles and enchants all who encounter her: the crowds drunk on beer and the succulent samba girls imported from Brazil and Cuba, as well as the "rich daddy's boys"—progeny of the city's customs brokers, hoteliers, restaurateurs, and senior government officials—who had snubbed her before her coronation; the older men who gush about the color of her eyes, as well as the newspaper poets who dedicate verses to her and publish them in the Sunday papers:

Evangelina the Second,
with Artemis's style:
Venus bitterly envies
The candor of your smile.

Across Heroic Veracruz
its people cheer and scream
Moved by the austere smile
of fair Evangelina their queen.

Looking at photos of this triumphant Evangelina—draped in costume necklaces and bracelets, silver-and-white frills, her hair in an elegant updo, feathers in her headdress and sequins on her dress—and then at images of the broken, crestfallen woman published six years later—no longer in gossip rags but in the crime pages of the newspapers, alongside the crooks and degenerates—it's impossible not to search for signs of a disturbed mind developing behind the radiant face: Is that a twinkle of evil cunning, perhaps, in the queen's eye? Isn't there a hint of weariness, or even strain, in the stiff smile plastered on her face? Isn't there something cruel about her indifference as she avoids looking into the photographer's lens? As she sat on her papier-mâché throne, her lowly subjects calling out to her over the hubbub of heckling, obscenities, and laughter, could Evangelina have already begun, even as early as then, to sense what the future had in store for her? Perhaps Mario de la Rosa was already on her mind during the festivities, while the "incredible voice" of Dulce, "the biggest singer of the moment," performed live, singing the ballad that would become—along with hits by songwriter Rafel Pérez Botja, sung by José José and Rocío Durcal—the anthem for codependency and emotional worthlessness, the defining zeitgeist of the eighties:

I'll be your lover or whatever it takes
I'll be what you ask me to be
I mean it, my love,
Do what you want with me
Queen, slave, or woman
Just let me come back to you.

On April 10, 1989, after her initial detention period was over, Evangelina Tejera Bosada was brought before Judge Rodríguez Moreno, who signed an order of imprisonment against the accused. "Upon discovering her true legal situation, the woman who murdered her children wept for the first time," wrote a correspondent for the *Diario de Xalapa*, relishing Tejera Bosada's suffering and her visible distress and agitation, which his "well-informed sources" put down to drug-withdrawal symptoms. J. P. de León, a journalist for *El Dictamen*, described the judge's ruling as "thorough and well founded," since the imprisonment order would make it hard for the defense attorney to invoke Article 418 from the then Code of Penal Procedure, which—in language yet to be acquainted with political correctness—allowed a criminal trial to be terminated "at the first indication that the accused is either insane, an idiot, an imbecile, or suffers from any other incapacity, infirmity, or mental abnormality."

Public opinion was divided: some speculated that Evangelina killed her sons because they cramped her style, others thought that she committed the crime in a jealous rage after discovering that De la Rosa had a new lover, and that she was now trying to pass for a madwoman to avoid a prison sentence. There were those who believed that Tejera Bosada had genuinely suffered a psychotic episode, brought on by her drug abuse, and a select few refused to believe that the young mother could have been capable of committing such a heinous act and suggested that the boys had been murdered by someone seeking revenge. Finally, there were whispers that the old Carnival Queen was part of a "narco-satanic" sect, a rumor that perhaps sprang from the exceedingly gory manner in which the boys, Jaime and Juan Miguel, were killed and mutilated, or perhaps simply because it was something of a hot topic at the time: in May 1983, every newspaper in the country reported on the arrest of the gang known as The Narcosatanists and the death of Adolfo de Jesús Constanzo, alias the Godfather, the leader of this criminal group–cum-satanic

sect, which not only trafficked drugs between Mexico and the United States but was also accused of the abduction, rape, and ritualistic murder of at least fifteen people.

Just a few days after Tejera Bosada was imprisoned in a high-security cell in the Ignacio Allende prison, Judge Rodríguez Moreno ordered the formation of a medical advisory board that would examine the defendant and determine whether she had a psychiatric disorder that exempted her from criminal punishment. Having assessed her, the medical experts concluded that Evangelina Tejera showed signs of "antisocial personality disorder, kleptomania, and an acute psychotic episode," and while they ruled out frontal lobe epilepsy, they did recommend to the judge that the defendant undergo specialized psychiatric and neurological examinations. Doctors David Reyes and Alberto Miranda were selected to carry out the first of these examinations, which began on May 8 at Veracruz General Hospital and concluded almost two months later with discouraging results for the defense: Evangelina's behavioral disorders were not the result of any kind of endocrine or brain pathology.

It's not clear what happened immediately after these two assessments; the press was no longer covering Evangelina Tejera's story. One has to access the criminal-trial records to find out what happened next: on March 7, 1990, almost a year after the crime was discovered, Judge Rodríguez ultimately determined the defendant to be mentally incapacitated and arranged for her to be admitted to the Orizaba Psychiatric Hospital "for as long as it takes for her to recover her mental health." The treatment seemed to work, as three years later, on November 16, 1993, Doctor Gregorio Pérez concluded that Tejera Bosada had fully recovered.

But the defendant did not get to enjoy her newfound freedom. She was detained at the doors of the hospital by a group of judicial police officers with a new arrest warrant, who drove her back to the Ignacio Allende prison in Veracruz to resume the trial for the voluntary manslaughter of her two children. The public—and, in particular, the team of lawyers led by Reyes Peralta—could not and would not let the crime go. Three years after the case reopened, Judge Samuel Baizabal Maldonado sentenced Evangelina to twenty-eight years of imprisonment and a fine of thirty-five pesos.

Using several different public defenders, Tejera Bosada did everything in her power to appeal this new ruling and avoid imprisonment, citing the violation of her legal rights—she had been put on trial twice for the same crime. Nonetheless, none of her attempts were successful. As far as Mexico's Supreme Court was concerned, the resumption of the trial immediately after Tejera Bosada's discharge from the psychiatric hospital was perfectly legal, since the evidence presented by the prosecution adequately demonstrated that her mental illness didn't begin until after she committed the crime. According to the Supreme Court judges who reviewed the dispute, the twenty-eight-year prison sentence imposed by Maldonado Baizabal in 1996 was fair and unappealable, since it had been proven beyond all reasonable doubt that when Evangelina Tejera beat her children against the floor and walls of her living room, dismembered their bodies, buried them in a pot, placed said pot on the balcony in plain view of half of Veracruz, and then walked around naked for several days in front of the windows of her National Lottery building apartment, she acted at all times "in full possession of her mental faculties."

Daniel, pimp: "I don't think she killed those boys . . . She wasn't a violent person . . . She was more of a party animal, a druggie—hard into her weed and coke, sure, but she wasn't crazy . . . At first I did believe she'd killed them, because there were times it seemed like those boys just got in the way of her highs, but then I thought, No, she wouldn't be capable of that, and definitely not chopping them into pieces . . . I was always over at her place; we'd all hang out there . . . Mario, Kayser, Guillo, Tiburcio, Picho, Cara de León; the boys would roll up and there'd be all sorts . . . Man, that was some world-class blow, like from back in the day, not the nasty shit they sell now. It came in sort of flakes, crystals almost . . . Cost about a grand a gram but it was like a turbocharger . . . There were always people in that apartment getting fucked up, drinking, dancing . . . And the kids, well, in their room, of course . . . Yeah, I saw them once or twice; they were little blond things, like her . . . personally I think Evangelina lost it afterward, after what she went through . . . I think it was the narcos who killed those kids, in revenge, because she and that dickhead De la Rosa snorted all the coke and spent all the money . . . I think that's why she never confessed to doing it but at the same time never ratted on whoever did. Because she'd rather live with the stigma than have the narcos come after her and kill her. And that's why she hooked up with that guy from Los Zetas cartel on the inside, to protect herself from her enemies . . ."

Evangelina's case didn't appear in the press again until 2007, a decade after her definitive sentence, when her name became linked to a character both feared and revered by the crime tabloid writers of the early aughts: Oscar Sentíes Alfonsín, better known as Güero Valli. Originally from Cosamaloapan and detained several times for robbery, possession of illegal arms, and crimes against public health, Sentíes Alfonsín was considered a dangerous prisoner, and suspected of being one of the principal drug smugglers into Veracruz's jails. He was also suspected, according to articles written by Lourdes López, César Augusto Vázquez Chagoya, and Miguel Ángel López Velasco, of being Tejera Bosada's new romantic partner. Apparently, they had met in jail in Pacho Viejo, Perote, where they were both transferred: Evangelina because of the constant clashes she provoked among the other female prisoners inside the Ignacio Allende, and Sentíes Alfonsín for organizing several rebellions at the Villa Aldama federal prison. For his repeated misbehavior, the authorities punished Güero Valli with the "carousel"—continuous transfer between penitentiaries—a strategy that supposedly prevented the purchase of "privileges." When they transferred Güero Valli from Perote to Amatlán, Evangelina Tejera went with him, and in May 2008 they were both part of the "chain" of prisoners sent to a brand-new prison in Coatzacoalcos. According to the journalist Miguel Ángel López Velasco (who wrote under the pseudonym Milo Vela until he was assassinated in June 2011, allegedly by members of organized crime) on the day of the prison's opening, Sentíes Alfonsín spoke to then-director of Social Rehabilitation for the state, Zeferino Tejeda Uscanga, to "push" the case for the early release of "his woman," who had served exactly half of her sentence. By then it was an open secret that the prisons in Veracruz were controlled, from the inside, by Los Zetas, who had recently broken away from the Gulf Cartel: they provided the inmates with drugs and grant privileges, like the ones Evangelina Tejera required in order to go on living in the Coatzacoalcos prison with Sentíes Alfonsín, despite the fact that she was now eligible for early release. And she enjoyed that privilege until October 2008, when Sentíes Alfonsín was stabbed to death by a fellow inmate in a punishment cell, where he'd been put for allegedly trying to organize another revolt.

As Michel Foucault points out in the book *I, Pierre Rivière, Having Slaughtered My Mother, My Sister, and My Brother: A Case of Parricide in the 19th Century*, every crime must serve some purpose to society because a completely gratuitous crime, one without any motive at all, is unimaginable. The community must instead come up with unique and singular causes for the crime, precluding any reflection on the structural conditions surrounding it and passing over connections between that crime and other cases from the same period. In Tejera Bosada's case, these would include the economic crisis, violence against women, the breakdown of the family, and Mexico's failed social security and child protection systems.

I've always been troubled by the contiguity that exists between the society pages and sensationalist "bleeding leads," and not only because these two sections are usually published close together in Veracruz's newspapers (often on facing pages, as if mirroring each other), but because both genres tend to present the subject matters of their "literature" as exceptional, one-off, unrepeatable events. First, the rise of a young woman to the status of Carnival Queen, a living symbol of the joy, vitality, and fruitfulness of Veracruz's people; then, her subsequent disgrace as the murderer of her own children, a mythical villain, a fairy-tale witch whose name is invoked by mothers all over Veracruz telling boys and girls to eat their vegetables, or else "Evangelina will come and punish you." Opposing yet complementary archetypes, masks that dehumanize flesh and blood women and become blank screens on which to project the desires, fears, and anxieties of a society that professes to be an enclave of tropical sensualism but deep down is profoundly conservative, classist, and misogynist.

Three decades after the double homicide that shook the people of Veracruz, the whereabouts of fair Evangelina are still unknown. Some accounts say she returned to the city and now lives as a recluse in a miserable downtown tenement, obese, ailing, and out of her mind. Other rumors have it that a family member employed her: in an optician's office, some say, or a medical laboratory, or a veterinary clinic. Some claim to have seen her in the luxury hotel resorts on the Riviera Maya, svelte, dripping in jewels, on the arm of the big bosses from Los Zetas, to whom it's said she must have turned for protection after Güero Valli's assassination.

And while the legend of her crime lives on in whispers, to this day it is still possible to walk to the top of Independencia, stand on the corner of Calle Melchor Ocampo, look up at the National Lottery building, and search its west facade for the balcony of apartment 501. Perhaps the constant flow of pedestrians along that street will prevent an inquisitive person from standing there for very long, but with a bit of luck, they'll still glimpse the yellow light that on some nights, for a matter of hours, goes on in that apartment. And perhaps a terrible thought will flash through their mind: that just like her children, the old Carnival Queen, the convicted murderer Evangelina Tejera Bosada, has herself become a ghost. ✦

ANOTHER BIRTH
Forough Farrokhzad
Translated from the PERSIAN by ELIZABETH T. GRAY, JR.

My whole being is a dark verse
that by repeating you in itself
will carry you to the dawn of eternal blossoming and growth
In this verse I sighed you
ah, in this verse
I grafted you to tree and water and fire

Maybe life
is a long street in which every day a woman with a basket passes by
Maybe life
is a rope with which a man hangs himself from a branch
Maybe life is a young child coming home from school

Maybe life is lighting a cigarette in the languid pause between
    making love and making love again
or the distracted gait of a passer-by
who lifts his hat from his head
and with a meaningless smile says to another passer-by, "Good morning"

Maybe life is that enclosed moment
in which my gaze annihilates itself in the pupils of your eyes
and in this there is a feeling that I will mix
with the moon's understanding and the acceptance of darkness

In a room the size of a loneliness
my heart
the size of a love
looks for simple excuses for happiness
to the beautiful wilting of the flowers in the vase
to the sapling you planted in the garden of our house
and to the song of the canaries
who sing the size of a window

Ah . . .
This is my lot
This is my lot
My lot
is a sky that the pulling of a curtain takes away from me
My lot is to descend an abandoned stairway
and join something rotting and in exile
My lot is a walk stained with grief in the garden of memories
and to die grieving for the voice that says to me:
"I love
your hands"

I bury my hands in the garden
I will grow, I know, I know, I know
and swallows will lay their eggs
in the hollow of my ink-stained fingers

I hang twin red cherries
over my ears as earrings
and stick dahlia petals on my fingernails
There is an alleyway where
the boys who were in love with me
with the same tousled hair and skinny necks and spindly legs
are still thinking of the innocent smiles of a girl who was carried away
one night
by the wind

There is an alleyway that my heart
has stolen from the neighborhoods of my youth

The journey of a form along the line of time
a form impregnating the barren line of time
a form conscious of an image
that returns from a feast in a mirror

And thus it is
that someone dies
and someone remains

No fisherman will find a pearl in the humble stream that pours into a pit

I
know a sad little fairy
who lives in an ocean
and plays her heart out softly, softly
on a pennywhistle
a sad little fairy
who dies with a kiss at night
and is born with a kiss at dawn

BORDER WALLS
Forough Farrokhzad
Translated from the PERSIAN by ELIZABETH T. GRAY, JR.

Now, again, in the silent night
barrier walls, border walls
grow tall like plants
guardians of the fields of my love

Now, again, the filthy hubbub of the city
like an agitated school of fish
decamps from the darkness of my shore
Now, again, the windows find themselves
pleasured by the touch of diffused scents
Now all the trees asleep in the garden slip out of their bark
and through thousands of pores the soil
inhales the dizzy particles of the moon

Now
come closer
and listen
to the disturbed beats of love
like the *tom-tom* of an African drum
that spreads chants through the tribe of my limbs

I sense
I know
the moment of prayer, which moment it is
Now all the stars
are making love with each other

Protected by the night I drift
from the end of all that is breeze
Protected by the night, with my heavy hair
I cascade madly
into your hands and I make a gift to you
of equatorial flowers from this young green tropical land

Come with me
Come with me to that star
to that star that for thousands of millennia
lies far from the frozen soil and empty scales of the Earth
And no one there
is afraid of light

On islands floating on the surface of the water, I breathe
I
I am looking for a piece of the vast sky
uncrowded by base thoughts

Come back to me
Come back to me
to the beginning of the body
to the fragrant center of a sperm
to the moment that I was created from you
Come back to me
I have remained incomplete because of you

Now the pigeons
take wing
above the peaks of my breasts
Now inside the cocoon of my lips
butterfly kisses contemplate flight
Now
the mehrāb of my flesh
is ready for love's worship

Come back to me
I have no words
because I love you
because "I love you" is a saying
that comes from the world of futilities
and worn-out things and repeated things
Come back to me
I have no words

Protected by the night
let me become pregnant with the moon
Let me be filled
by small drops of rain
by not-yet-developed hearts
by the form of unborn babies
Let me be filled
Maybe my love
will be the cradle for another Jesus

THE SMILE
Dahlia de la Cerda
Translated from the SPANISH by HEATHER CLEARY & JULIA SANCHES
ILLUSTRATION BY Nicole Rifkin

THIS STORY CONTAINS GRAPHIC DESCRIPTIONS OF SEXUAL VIOLENCE

CAME NORTH ON the Beast. Nothing left for me back home. Not anymore, anyway. Came up looking for a future. Heard there was work in the maquiladoras near the border and that while I was there, I might as well hop over to the other side. Gringo dream, ya sabes. I rode the Beast 'cause it's free: all you do is take off, run, run, jump, and úpale, you're on. Course, only if you're lucky and get a good grip, if not the Beast will crush you with its steel hooves and best-case scenario it kills you, or else you're lame for good. But life's a gamble and I went all in, what the fuck.

I didn't have a pot to piss in back home. I was dirt poor and totally screwed—slept in a hammock, lived in flip-flops, ate fish scraps for every meal. No future there. Zip. And nowhere to look for one either. No joke. My days went more or less like this: wake up, fish with my apá, head to the docks to sell our catch, then back to the beach for the sunset. Sounds pretty sweet for one day, or for a vacation or whatever, but trust me that shit's not so hot. I wanted to see the world, buy something to listen to music on. To dance, have a little fun. What I didn't want was to be stuck looking at the same sand, the same waves, the same sunset until I died. But I got the math wrong: life's a bitch.

Back home they called me La Negra. I'm Black, so what. All black maize, tumbao, and a mess of curly hair. Afro, they called me at the factory. Here at the maquiladora, I'm Chiki, la chiquita. 'Cause I'm not just Black, I'm tiny, too. Short, Black, with messy curls. Look, here comes the walking microphone, they'd say. Those bitches always had their claws out. Then up north I confused everybody. They didn't get how I could be Mexican, as Mexican as I am Black. They thought I'd come out mulatita 'cause my amá cheated on my apá with some gringo rapper, or that a Black woman left me on the beach and my family adopted me. Please. I'm more Mexican than nopales. Mexica negrita. Brown sugar, the gringos called me when I sold them fish on a stick.

The border isn't what you think, or what people say it is. The border is a ravenous monster. A bottomless pit that feeds on work, sex, drugs, and women. I had no idea. All I'd been told was there was work in Juárez at the factories and maquiladoras, that stuff was intense up there, ragers every fucking day, and look, I'm just saying all that shit got my head spinning.

I didn't tell a soul. Just took off one day. Rode up here, dreams and all. Juárez is just one big ranch, far as I can tell. A ranch crawling with dudes in oversize cowboy hats and trucks that make you say, Those fuckers are totally narcos. And boots hanging from power lines. Every place has its own footwear: on the coast they've got flip-flops, in the country I saw sneakers hung by the laces, and here it's cowboy boots. Cracks me up. People, man, we're a fucking riot. They put up pink crosses here, too, in memory of the dead girls of Juárez. There are more signs for desaparecidas than dances, that's what I was told.

On the Beast I met this awesome chick from Colombia. She had a shit ton of cumbia on her phone and gave me an earbud so we could listen together. Whenever the train slowed down and it wasn't too hilly, we danced. You heard me, right there on top of the train, cheating death. We were riding halfway across the country on la ruta de la muerte, so it's not like we weren't already playing with fire. Me and the Colombian danced real nice, I remember, pure cumbia, real sabrosito. It was like cheating death and not falling into the hands of narcos, rapists, and pimps. But that was real death cheating. When we danced on top of the train we were celebrating the fact that death didn't have shit on us, at least not that day. With cumbia, there was no death, only dance. The Colombian chick left me in Juaritos and went off in search of the American Dream. I moved in with my aunt, who lived in a tiny room on the outskirts of the city. She's the one who twisted my arm. What kind of life do you expect down there, you're not about to turn into a mermaid, move in with me up here. And I did.

Working at the maquiladora was like going to school but different. I had the night shift: in at 4 P.M. and out at 4 A.M., when the roosters aren't singing, but the vultures are. Sometimes the maquiladora looks like prison: all of us in khaki, busting ass, making shit at full speed, pushing for a productivity bonus, busting our asses for a few hours of overtime and some scratch to pay into the tanda, busting our asses for a day off so we can go out and party.

I was having a blast. I knew working at a maquiladora was risky 'cause everybody just knows by word of mouth that all the desaparecidas are maquilocas. That's what they called the women who worked at the factories, maquilocas. Said we hooked up with truckers and slutted around, but it's not true, or maybe it is. Either way, it stung when dudes called us maquilocas. Fuck yeah I was loca. I worked my ass off and deserved to go a little crazy. I liked to party, I liked to dress sexy and paint my lips red. I hung around with guys from work and made out with dudes at parties. I wasn't into cantinas, though. If people weren't dancing, it wasn't for me. I love music, guys, and grinding. So sue me. I worked my ass off, for real. Zero vacation days, double output, double shifts and shit, all so I could pull on a pair of high-heeled boots, tight jeans, and a denim jacket and party till dawn with two or three guys. I only ever drank a couple of beers. I'm seventeen. Does being a maquiloca mean I deserve what happened to me? Was I asking for it? Do you really think I'd be asking for it? I spent a whole week cheating death while dancing cumbia. Please, mijo.

The funniest part was that when they killed me—did they kill me?—I wasn't even out partying. I remember I'd thrown on a shirt with Los Tigres del Norte on it that day, plus a black skirt that went to my knees and a pair of shell-toe sneakers. Ridiculous, I know, but I'd been working nonstop for two months to buy a phone and a ticket for the VIP section at Intocable and I just couldn't be bothered. I had four different tandas going, I was saving up. So I caught a bus headed to the city, 'cause that way it'd be cheaper to get home. But something went wrong. Very fucking wrong. When I got on there were like ten other girls, but one by one they got off until I was left alone with the driver. Christ. Just thinking about it makes my hands sweat, just like they did that night, they became the ocean, they were sweating and I was sweating, scared to death. El Poder del Norte was playing on my headphones but the lead's nasal voice couldn't distract me from my paranoia—or was it a premonition? I still don't know when the driver, that piece of shit, went off route. I started praying,

I prayed to God it was a shortcut, that it was just a more direct way back, but no, all of a sudden there was nothing out there, just desert and dark. I'm fucked, I thought. Fucking fucked. Panic took hold of me and I started screaming for him to let me off the bus, where the hell was he taking me, on his mother's life and his fucking daughter's life he'd better not lay a fucking finger on me. The piece of shit just laughed. He stopped the bus. I was curled up in a ball, sobbing, cursing. I heard him step out and saw the lights of a patrol car. I screamed, I screamed my lungs out, I called for help, I begged, but those dirtbags pretended they couldn't hear me and let him drive on. We headed farther into the desert. And then he braked, hard. He opened the door and four other pieces of shit climbed in. You want me to tell it?

They raped me, all five of them. They took turns. Tied my hands and feet, burned me with cigarettes, beat me until they got tired. They'd let me go just so they could hunt me down again. They bit my breasts. They'd let me go and I'd run as hard as I could, but they were faster and stronger. Whenever one caught up to me, he'd grab me by the hair and throw me down on the sand. Then he'd kick my face, my chest. Viciously.

I'd heard lots of things, that they used girls for sado porn and satanic rituals for bored gringos. But no. None of that. They didn't film shit and they weren't gringos, they were Mexican dudes, could've been your cousin or my dad, normal guys, not yuppies or foreigners. I don't know why they do it, I don't, but if I know one thing it's this: they enjoy it. They liked watching me cry and beg. It was in their eyes, in their grunts of pleasure. Fucking assholes, pieces of shit, motherfuckers. They'd play at suffocating me with a red bandanna and when they saw I was on my last legs they'd let me go, then fuck with me all over again.

Between all the dicks and hands I couldn't tell how long they were at it, but I was all fucked up, beaten to shit, bruises on top of bruises and burns on top of burns. They raped me with their filthy cocks and their nasty fingers and with something made of metal. When they finally got bored, they left me for dead in the middle of the desert.

Little by little, the darkness turned light. I opened my eyes and saw El Charro Negro standing right next to me. So La Santa Muerte comes for me and she's a fucking dude, I thought. But no, it wasn't her. I realized it wasn't Death because the guy took a bite out of my neck. That's right, motherfucker bit me. Then he threw me over his shoulder and that's the last thing I remember.

I had a fever or something worse. Maybe I died and came back, it was a trip and I had these—whoops broken record—trippy visions or like memories. I remembered how when my siblings and I were little, we used to pee the bed. Super funny, I don't know why I remembered that or dreamed it, really, but for a while there, we were real little pissers. We were synchronized, pissing the bed at the exact same time, totally supernatural. My parents tried everything and nothing worked. We even came up with a couple of prevention strategies, but no dice. In the end, my apá had no choice but to give us baths in the morning so we didn't reek when we went to school. The part that stressed me out was that I was older, twelve already, and I was flirting with this boy, so I thought, What if we run off and I piss all over him on our first night together? He'll dump me right back on my doorstep. I was in the middle of this childhood soap opera when I woke up. It didn't take me long to figure out I was in a freaking cave in the middle of the desert. At least I was alive. I cheated death, I thought. What I didn't realize was–I am death.

I saw the sun coming up and figured I'd step outside to catch a few rays, check the scene, see what's what. Bad idea. The second the light hit my skin I felt like I was on fire, I fucking started giving off smoke, motherfuck, so I scrambled back inside. The next few days were awful. Nothing compared to my rape and murder, but definitely still shitty. My skin started decomposing, but it didn't just smell like rot, it actually started falling off. In freaking strips. All my hair fell out. And I puked. I started puking up all my organs– stomach, intestines, kidneys, liver, pancreas, I shit you not. I watched the whole thing with these eyes that no worm will ever eat. I watched my damn intestines come out my mouth. They still tasted like tacos al pastor. Seriously, I even tugged them a little to make it go faster. My liver tasted like blood, like fresh blood. I was into it. My pancreas was kinda sweet, like baby's milk. My heart? I didn't spit that out, God knows why.

After puking up all my organs and losing my hair, I died again. I don't know what to tell you. The whole thing seems like a weird-ass trip, but when I woke up I was me. Like before. No cuts or bruises, no pain, no nothing: there I was, motherfucking Chiki in all my splendor, but buck naked, or almost. All I had on was a black T-shirt. Those pieces of shit ditched my clothes who the fuck knows where, fucking assholes. So I waited for it to get dark, right, and I went looking for El Charro Negro, the fucker who bit me. Dude owed me an explanation or two. I started walking through the desert and I swear to God I could see totally fine in the dark, like I was wearing those ultrared goggles or some shit. Infrared? Anyway, it rocked. Before I knew it, I stumbled on a freaking camper van in the middle of the desert. I knocked on the door real cute and when I had the dude in front of me I was like, What the fuck, man?

El Charro Negro said this fucking hilarious thing, said I'd cheated death and found my way back. Apparently those pieces of shit hadn't killed me all the way, they'd just left me out there dying and then he put some weird spell on me to catch my last breath and keep it and make it eternal. My take is that matter isn't created or destroyed, it just gets transformed, right, what the fuck are you laughing at, I might look dumb but I finished high school, asshole. El Charro told me my body could cure itself now, but that it needed blood to do it. Not human blood, 'cause the lines get crossed or some shit and you end up covered in hives. Animal blood can help our bodies regenerate and fix whatever injury. First you decompose, then you rise from the ashes dancing cumbia. Killer. He also told me about how my eyesight was like supercharged now, how I could smell and hear better, and had superhuman strength. I must be tripping, I thought. But no, man. It was real. Maybe that horrible shit I went through made me a martyr and now God was playing catch-up with these superpowers, or maybe it was life giving me a chance to get even. But same as how God didn't give scorpions wings, he gave us this one fucking weakness:

the sun. A mega motherfucking allergy to the sun. So I have to make my moves at night.

Long story short, El Charro Negro filled me in on the whole undead thing, the mutation of survival. He told me how raven's blood tastes bitter, how if we want to go in somewhere we have to be invited, ha, you should've seen me standing at the door of these shops in Juaritos asking the girls, Hey, can I come in? All so I could buy some freaking threads. And a few of them were real bitches and answered like, Yeah, or, No, but I needed them to say the whole thing, You can come in, or, You may enter, or whatever. It was a major hassle but I got what I was looking for: a Tigres del Norte shirt just like the one I had on the night those pieces of shit went way the fuck overboard.

I don't know how the hell I managed, but I used my feminine wiles to convince El Charro to help me get revenge. Not that it was all that hard. Did I mention dude had a hobby that was like sweet and terrifying at the same time? He collected the bones of murdered women and put them where they could be found. I asked him why, with his superpowers and everything, he never stopped the killers or killed them or did anything to them. He told me he was waiting for a woman to do that part.

Dude was a saint, went all over Juaritos with me so I could buy a black denim skirt and shell-toe sneakers. I saw my face on a poster. MISSING, it said. It made me sad as fuck to picture my family out there searching for me and my aunt counting how many days it'd been. No one had heard from me in six months, they had no idea if I was dead or alive. I gave into temptation and drew a speech bubble on one of the posters that said, "Pieces of shit fucked me, but I'm alive and I'm coming for them." El Charro smiled in a way I hadn't seen before. I went into a public restroom, threw on my Los Tigres del Norte shirt, black skirt, and sneakers, and painted my lips red. I looked in the mirror. I couldn't see my reflection but I knew it was me. The same me who'd walked out of the maquiladora that morning. The exact same person. I was dead but the desert hadn't devoured me, it had spat me out, puked me up. I smiled. I walked out of the bathroom and a cumbia tune by Grupo Cañaveral was playing. I stopped and danced the way I'd danced with the Colombian chick on top of the Beast, one of those moments when you think you're cheating death but don't realize the motherfucking joke's on you.

El Charro Negro walked me to the bus stop. I recognized the number right away: 495. The bus slowed and I got on with some other chicks. The driver didn't even notice me. I sat all the way in the back, hidden enough so he couldn't really see me but not so much that he wouldn't know I was there. Déjà vu. He went off route, pulled over for a patrol car. Headed into the desert, stopped. The four pieces of shit were there waiting. I went out to meet them. One of the bastards recognized me immediately. I guess the Afro and the Los Tigres del Norte shirt gave me away. "Is this a fucking joke?" he asked the driver. I didn't give them a chance to say shit. Not one fucking word. I walked up to them, real slow, and saw the panic on their faces. One of them pissed himself, those fuckers can dish it out but they can't take it. I was scared, our bodies remember. But I swallowed my fear and smiled, baring my fangs. ✦

Evan M. Cohen

CONTRIBUTORS

Nada Alic is the author of the collection *Bad Thoughts*, which will be published by Vintage in July 2022. She lives in Los Angeles. ✦ Larry Buchanan is a graphics editor at the *New York Times*, where part of his job is to make maps. He currently lives on a small island off the coast of the United States. ✦ Dahlia de la Cerda was born in Aguascalientes, Mexico. She is the author of *Perras de reserva* and the codirector of the feminist collective Morras Help Morras. In 2019, she won the prestigious Premio Nacional de Cuento Joven Comala. ✦ Jos Charles is the author of *Safe Space, feeld*, and *a Year & other poems*, forthcoming from Milkweed in March 2022. She is currently a Ph.D. student at UC Irvine and resides in Long Beach, California. ✦ Don Mee Choi, born in Seoul, is a 2021 MacArthur and Guggenheim fellow. Her translation of Kim Hyesoon's next collection, *Phantom Pain Wings*, is forthcoming from New Directions in 2023. ✦ Nicole Claveloux's comics have appeared in English in *The Green Hand and Other Stories* and the forthcoming *Dead Season and Other Stories*, both published by New York Review Comics. She lives in France. ✦ Heather Cleary has translated novels by Brenda Lozano, María Ospina, Betina González, Mario Bellatin, and Sergio Chejfec, among others. A member of the Cedilla & Co. translation collective and founding editor of the bilingual *Buenos Aires Review*, she teaches at Sarah Lawrence College. ✦ Evan M. Cohen is an illustrator, animator, and comic book artist living in the Midwest. His work has appeared in the *New York Times*, *The New Yorker*, *Bloomberg Businessweek*, and more. ✦ Ama Asantewa Diaka is a storyteller. She is the author of the chapbook *You Too Will Know Me* and the poetry collection *Woman, Eat Me Whole*, which will be published by Ecco in April 2022. ✦ Maria Clara Drummond is a Brazilian writer and journalist currently based in Lisbon. She is the author of *A festa é minha e eu choro se eu quiser* and *A realidade devia ser proibida. Role Play* is her third novel. ✦ Kristin Dykstra is a writer, literary translator, and professor. Her translations include books by Marcelo Morales, Juan Carlos Flores, Tina Escaja, and others. She is the principal English translator of Reina María Rodríguez's *The Winter Garden Photograph*, which won the 2020 PEN Award for Poetry in Translation. ✦ Diana Ejaita is a textile designer, artist, and illustrator based in Berlin and Lagos. Her work has appeared in the *New York Times* and on the cover of *The New Yorker*. ✦ Helena Fagertun is a Swedish writer, editor, and translator. She has translated authors such as Kate Zambreno, Mary MacLane, and Sally Rooney. ✦ Forough Farrokhzad (1934–1967) was an Iranian poet, filmmaker, screenwriter, and painter. During her lifetime, she published four poetry collections: *The Captive*, *The Wall*, *Rebellion*, and *Another Birth*. She also translated the work of George Bernard Shaw and Henry Miller, and made a groundbreaking documentary, *The House Is Black*, about a leper colony in northeastern Iran. ✦ Elizabeth T. Gray, Jr. is the author of the poetry collection *Series | India*. Her translations from classical and contemporary Persian include *Wine and Prayer: Eighty Ghazals* from the Díwán of Hafiz, *The Green Sea of Heaven: Fifty Ghazals from the Díwán of Hafiz*, and *Iran: Poems of Dissent*. ✦ Maja Haderlap is a Slovenian Austrian writer and translator. She was awarded the Ingeborg-Bachmann-Preis and the Rauriser Literaturpreis for her debut novel, *Angel of Oblivion*. ✦ Terrance Hayes's most recent publications include *American Sonnets for My Past and Future Assassin*, which won the 2019 Hurston/Wright Legacy Award for Poetry, and *To Float in the Space Between: Drawings and Essays in Conversation with Etheridge Knight*, which was the winner of the 2019 Pegasus Award for Poetry Criticism. Hayes is a professor of English at New York University. ✦ Steven Heller is the co-chair and cofounder of SVA's MFA Design program. He is the author or editor of over two hundred books on design, typography, political satire, and popular culture. A former columnist for the *New York Times Book Review*, he writes The Daily Heller for *Print*. ✦ Sophie Hughes has translated writers such as Enrique Vila-Matas, Alia Trabucco Zerán, and José Revueltas. She won the Queen Sofía Cultural Institute's 2021 Translation Prize for her translation of Fernanda Melchor's *Hurricane Season*. ✦ Born in Gutu, Zimbabwe in 1993, Kudzanai-Violet Hwami currently lives and works in the UK. In 2019, Hwami presented work at the 58th Venice Biennale as part of the Zimbabwe Pavilion, the youngest artist to participate. Also in 2019, Hwami mounted her first institutional solo exhibition at Gasworks, London. In September 2021, she had her first solo exhibition, "When You Need Letters for Your Skin," at Victoria Miro. Recent group exhibitions include "Ubuntu: A Lucid Dream," at the Palais de Tokyo, Paris, France. ✦ Leslie Jamison is the author of *The Empathy Exams*, *The Recovering: Intoxication and Its Aftermath*, and *Make It Scream, Make It Burn*. She teaches at Columbia University and lives in Brooklyn with her daughter. ✦ Sawako Kabuki is an illustrator and animator based in Tokyo. ✦ Mieko Kawakami is the author of the internationally best-selling novel *Breasts and Eggs* and *Heaven*. She has received numerous prestigious literary awards in Japan, including the Akutagawa Prize, the Tanizaki Prize, and the Murasaki Shikibu Prize. She lives in Tokyo. ✦ Kim Hyesoon has published thirteen poetry collections, including *Poor Love Machine*, *A Drink of Red Mirror*, and *Autobiography of Death*, for which she received the 2019 International Griffin Poetry Prize. She lives in Seoul, where she is the honorary professor of Seoul Institute of Arts. ✦ Catherine Lacey is the author of four books, most recently *Pew*, which won the 2021 Young Lions Fiction Award. She is the recipient of a Guggenheim Fellowship and a Whiting Award. Her fifth book, *Biography of X*, will be published by Farrar, Straus and Giroux in 2023. ✦ Franz Lang is an artist and illustrator based in London. ✦ Tess Lewis is a writer and translator from French and German. Her essays and reviews have appeared in *Bookforum*, *The Hudson Review*, the *Wall Street Journal*, and elsewhere. She won the PEN Translation Prize for her translation of Maja Haderlap's novel *Angel of Oblivion* and is a 2021–22 Berlin Prize Fellow at the American Academy in Berlin. ✦ Ada Limón is the author of six books of poetry, including *The Carrying*, which won the National Book Critics Circle Award for Poetry. She lives in Lexington, Kentucky, where she writes, teaches remotely, and hosts the critically acclaimed poetry podcast *The Slowdown*. Her new book of poetry, *The Hurting Kind*, is forthcoming from Milkweed in

May 2022. ✦ Lin Yu-Hsuan (林佑軒) is a writer and translator who holds a master's degree from Paris 8 University. His work has been included in several collections and chosen for the Taiwanese literature translation project. ✦ Eve Liu is an illustrator based in New York. Recently, she has been experimenting with animated art and needle crafts. ✦ Rachel Mannheimer was born and raised in Anchorage, Alaska, and lives in New Haven, Connecticut, where she works as a literary scout and as a senior editor for *The Yale Review*. Her first book, *Earth Room*, was selected by Louise Glück as the inaugural winner of the Bergman Prize and is forthcoming from Changes Press in April 2022. ✦ Lorenzo Mattotti is an Italian illustrator and cartoonist whose work has been published in *The New Yorker*, *Vogue*, and Louis Vuitton's *Travel Book: Vietnam*. In 2019, he released his first animated feature, *The Bears' Famous Invasion of Sicily*. He lives and works in Paris. ✦ Ella May is an artist from Krasnoyarsk, Russia, currently based in Thailand. ✦ María Medem started producing zines after studying fine arts in Seville, Spain, where she still lives and works as an illustrator. Her work has appeared in anthologies such as *Now*, *Cold Cube*, and *Colorama Clubhouse*. ✦ Fernanda Melchor is widely recognized as one of the most exciting new voices in Mexican literature. Her novel *Hurricane Season* has been translated into more than thirty languages and won the Anna Seghers Award. Her latest novel is *Paradais*. ✦ Moonassi is an illustrator from Seoul. ✦ Marcelo Morales is the author of *The World as Presence / El mundo como ser*. His previous books include *El mundo como objeto*, *Materia*, and a novel, *La espiral*. English translations from his newest works have appeared recently in *Two Lines Journal*,

Seedings, and *Mantis*, among others. ✦ Ottessa Moshfegh is the author of four novels, including *My Year of Rest and Relaxation*, and the short story collection *Homesick for Another World*. ✦ Sayaka Murata is the author of many books, including *Earthlings* and *Convenience Store Woman*, winner of the Akutagawa Prize. Murata has been named a *Freeman's* "Future of New Writing" author and a *Vogue Japan* Woman of the Year. ✦ Donald Nicholson-Smith's translations include the works of Jean-Patrick Manchette, Guy Debord, Henri Lefebvre, Antonin Artaud, and Guillaume Apollinaire. Born in Manchester, England, he has lived in New York City for many years. ✦ Dorthe Nors is one of the most distinguished contemporary Danish writers. In addition to her two short story collections, *Karate Chop* and *Wild Swims*, she has published one novella and five novels. Nors's work has appeared in *The New Yorker*, *Harper's*, and *Boston Review*, among many others. ✦ Chinelo Okparanta is the author of *Under the Udala Trees* and *Happiness, Like Water*. Her honors include an O. Henry Prize, the NAACP Image Award in Fiction, and the Young Lions Fiction Award, among others. Her second novel, *Harry Sylvester Bird*, is forthcoming from Mariner in July 2022. ✦ Zoë Perry's translations of contemporary Brazilian literature have appeared in *The New Yorker*, *Granta*, and *The Paris Review*. She is a founding member of The Starling Bureau, a literary translators' collective, and was selected for a Banff International Translation Centre residency for her translation of Emilio Fraia's *Sevastopol*. ✦ Tiana Reid is a writer and academic from Toronto. She is currently a postdoctoral research associate in the department of English at Brown University. ✦ Aaron Reiss is a freelance researcher, journalist, and cartographer.

His multimedia work has appeared in *The New Yorker*, the *New York Times*, and *This American Life*, among others. ✦ Nicole Rifkin is an award-winning illustrator based in New York City. ✦ Chloe Garcia Roberts is the author of *The Reveal*. Her translations include Li Shangyin's *Derangements of My Contemporaries: Miscellaneous Notes*, which was awarded a PEN/Heim Translation Fund Grant. She lives outside Boston, and works as the deputy editor of *Harvard Review*. ✦ Margaret Ross is the author of *A Timeshare*. She teaches at the University of Chicago, where she is a Harper-Schmidt Fellow. ✦ Julia Sanches is the author of more than a dozen translations from Spanish, Portuguese, and Catalan into English. Her translations and writing have appeared in *Granta*, *The Paris Review Daily*, and *The Common*, among others. Born in Brazil, she now lives in Providence, Rhode Island. ✦ Born in Istanbul to Iranian parents, Solmaz Sharif is the author of *Look*. Her work has appeared in *Harper's*, *The Paris Review*, the *New York Times*, and others. Her second poetry collection, *Customs*, will be published by Graywolf in March 2022. ✦ Trine Søndergaard is a Danish photo-based artist. Søndergaard has received the Albert Renger-Patzsch Prize and a three-year working grant from the Danish Arts Foundation. Søndergaard's work has been featured in many international group and solo exhibitions, most recently at The Royal Danish Library, Gammel Holtegaard, and Gothenburg Museum of Art. ✦ Ginny Tapley Takemori has translated works by more than a dozen Japanese writers, including Ryu Murakami. She lives at the foot of a mountain in eastern Japan. ✦ Saskia Vogel is a novelist, screenwriter, and Swedish-to-English translator of authors such as Johannes Anyuru, Balsam Karam, and Karolina Ramqvist. Her debut novel, *Permission*, has been published in five languages. She will be Princeton University's translator in residence for the fall 2022 semester. ✦ Katharina Volckmer was born in Germany in 1987. She lives in London, where she works for a literary agency. *The Appointment* is her first novel. ✦ Caroline Waight is an award-winning literary translator who works in Danish, German, and Norwegian. Her recent translations include Siri Ranva Hjelm Jacobsen's *Island* and Sayragul Sauytbay and Alexandra Cavelius's *The Chief Witness*. Her translation of Caroline Albertine Minor's *The Lobster's Shell* will be published by Granta in March 2022. ✦ Isabelle Wenzel lives and works in Wuppertal, Germany. Her works have been exhibited in the Netherlands Photo Museum, Fotografisk Center, and Galerie Bart, where she has collaborated on multiple solo and group exhibitions since 2010. ✦ Hitomi Yoshio is an associate professor of global Japanese literary and cultural studies at Waseda University. Her translations of Mieko Kawakami's work have appeared in *Granta*, *Monkey Business*, *The Penguin Book of Japanese Short Stories*, and others. ✦ Kate Zambreno is the author most recently of the novel *Drifts* and *To Write as If Already Dead*, a study of Hervé Guibert. ✦

Visit
and
to
MAGAZINE

WHEN WAS THE LAST TIME YOU FELT OR DID ECSTASY?

The last time I did ecstasy was at a friend's fortieth birthday party, which turned out to be more of a low-key gathering, and by that I mean I was the only person there on drugs. I spent the entire night trying to make small talk and seem normal, and did my best to hide my overwhelming sense of unconditional love for everyone there. —Nada Alic

The one time I tried ecstasy was in college with some girlfriends at a dive bar in Morningside Heights. It didn't work for me. I was on too many psychotropic medications. I've never tried again. No interest . . . —Ottessa Moshfegh

I last felt ecstasy in the middle of my living room, with my headphones on and a song by Lalo Rodríguez on full blast. *Devórame otra vez. Ven, devórame otra vez.* Dancing alone to salsa music is the perfect revenge. —Fernanda Melchor

After months, I was finally able to go to a market to eat my favorite food: gorditas stuffed with spicy green chili sauce and potatoes. When I took the first bite, I almost cried. —Dahlia de la Cerda

I feel ecstasy when I'm in a lucid dream. It's a space where anything you're longing for can be experienced, whether it's flying, or falling, or touch, all in a higher resolution than real life. —Mieko Kawakami

When I wrote a story about my own desire to kill and gave language to the dangerous unconscious feelings that lay dormant within me. —Sayaka Murata

A phone call today that went long and felt short left me floating. —Catherine Lacey

Dancing with my four-year-old daughter to that immortal Guns N' Roses epic, "November Rain." Her new favorite song. We make up dances based on her favorite things: the Noodle Dance, the Minotaur Dance, the Dill Havarti Dance. Dancing with her feels like discovering the fourth state of matter. —Leslie Jamison